Wiff and
Dirty George

Wiff and
Dirty George

The Z.E.B.R.A. Incident

Stephen R. Swinburne

BOYDS MILLS PRESS
HONESDALE, PENNSYLVANIA

Acknowledgments

Thanks to my Middlebury writing group, including Peter Lourie, Kirke Hart, Carolyn Craven, Ted Scheu, Barbara Seuling, Anna Dibble, and Sara Thurber Marshall.

Thanks to Keith Schoch and his 4th grade class in Bedminster Township School in New Jersey. I'm grateful to my English cousins—Dave and Erica—who read the manuscript. Thanks, also, for the thoughtful comments from my friend Debra Kaiser.

Nan, you loved reading a good adventure. You would have liked this one.

Text copyright © 2010 by Stephen R. Swinburne
All rights reserved
Printed in the United States of America
First edition

Library of Congress Cataloging-in-Publication Data

Swinburne, Stephen R.
  Wiff and Dirty George / Stephen R. Swinburne. — 1st ed.
      p. cm.
  Summary: In 1969 London, twelve-year-old friends Wiff and Dirty George set out to stop a master criminal from taking over England.
  ISBN 978-1-59078-755-7 (alk. paper)
[1. Adventure and adventurers—Fiction. 2. Criminals—Fiction. 3. Friendship—Fiction. 4. Mystery and detective stories. 5. Great Britain—History—Elizabeth II, 1952—Fiction.] I. Title.
  PZ7.S98135 Wif [Fic]—dc22   2009052214

Boyds Mills Press, Inc.
815 Church Street
Honesdale, Pennsylvania 18431

10 9 8 7 6 5 4 3 2

Oi, mate, congratulations!
You've found the address for *Wiff and Dirty George*!
Come visit us at www.wiffanddirtygeorge.com.
And dont forget to stop by www.steveswinburne.com.

To Heather, always—you said "Yes" and it has made all the difference in my life.

And to my girls, Hayley and Devon—I'll always remember your voices calling from the back seat of the car, "Tell us another Wiff and Dirty George story, Dad!"

Wiff and
Dirty George

The Z.E.B.R.A. Incident

1

Where and When
Early train to London, June 1969

Who
William ("Wiff") King,
George ("Dirty George") Potts,
and other passengers

Sound
Clickety-clack, clickety-clack, clickety-clack

"**M**e trousers are falling down!" cried Dirty George.

"Mine, too!" said Wiff.

"What's going on?"

"It's mad!" said Wiff.

Wiff checked his wristwatch. 7:25 a.m. Exactly. The train to Paddington Station had just crawled to a stop when every zipper unzipped, every buckle unbuckled, every button unbuttoned.

The railway car burst into bedlam. Handbags yawned wide. Briefcases sprung open. Fountain pens zoomed by Wiff's nose. Passengers shoved and struggled to grab their trousers and skirts. Dirty George had never seen so many pairs of pink polka-dot undies. Eyeglasses, cuff links, hairpins, and brooches hurtled to the floor. Belts curled around ankles like snakes.

A weird energy force had invaded the train, pulling everything downward.

Dirty George tried to yank up his trousers.

"Here, use this!" Wiff dug out some rope from his rucksack and tossed it to Dirty George. Then he wrenched the rope that held up his own trousers.

"What's that whirring noise?"

"It's coming from over there," said Wiff, pointing to the luggage rack five rows ahead.

At that moment, the door to car number 3 swung open and in stepped a large rabbit. The rabbit straddled a seat and blew a silver whistle dangling from its neck. The passengers looked up.

"Say *cheese!*"

A white flash filled car number 3 as the man in the rabbit suit snapped a photo. Then he reached above the luggage rack, grabbed a small silver disk, and dashed through the train's open door. The speakers filled the railroad car with the sound of a maniacal laugh.

"Crikey, who was *that?*" said Dirty George.

"I don't know, but c'mon," said Wiff. "Let's chase that rabbit!"

"Wiff, do we have to?"

"C'mon, mate, let's see what he's up to." Wiff squeezed through the crowded car to the exit.

If there was one thing Wiff and Dirty George could do, it was run. They excelled at running. If they took a class in running, they'd get A's. When school bullies threatened to pummel you because you had no parents (Wiff) or wallop you because you were poor and smelled of socks and old fish (Dirty George), you found your legs.

The boys ducked through the passenger-car door. They spotted the rabbit escaping along a deserted part of the platform. Wiff dug out a length of rope. The boys tugged the straps on their rucksacks and took off like sprinters.

Wiff tied a slipknot on the run. He'd practiced tying knots while running a hundred times before. Ever since his hands could grasp, Wiff had messed about with rope. Wiff grew up believing that when your parents are tragically killed while watching a lasso demonstration at a Texas rodeo, you never—*ever*—want to find yourself trapped by a rope. He practiced tying and untying knots every day, every spare moment. He was the best.

The boys caught up with the rabbit at the end of the platform. Wiff flung the noose. The knot snagged the rabbit's arm, and the boys planted their feet and tugged. The rabbit jerked to a halt. He spun to face his pursuers and, gripping the rope with one hand, pulled both boys toward him

"Crikey, Wiff! It's *Super-Rabbit*. Now what?"

It wasn't the first time Wiff had landed in a sticky situation. Nan, Wiff's grandmother, pleaded with him to think before he leaped. But Wiff kept leaping. And his run-ins with neighborhood ruffians and school thugs earned him black eyes and a thin white scar above his upper lip.

For an instant, Wiff thought how easy it would be to release the rope and run. But he'd saved his pennies to buy this good strand of double-braided nylon rope, and he wasn't about to lose it.

Wiff and Dirty George leaned back on their heels and tugged with everything they had, but the rabbit dragged them closer. When they'd reached arm's length, the rabbit flashed a smile of daggerlike teeth.

"Looks like the rabbit's outsmarted the foxes, eh, lads?"

"Mister, we only wanted to have a look at that . . . that silver disk," said Wiff.

"Shut up, you cheeky tykes," said the rabbit. "You're lucky I'm in a good humor, 'cause if I ever see the likes of you two again . . ."

The man whipped off his rabbit mask. Wiff and Dirty George stared into a pair of menacing eyes. Gray-black whiskers and an untamable mass of greasy black hair framed the man's twisted smile. The boys recoiled at the villain's teeth and vile breath.

"I'll have your throats!" said the rabbit, with a wicked grin. He held Wiff's rope up to his mouth. He sliced it cleanly in one bite, sprang from the platform, scuttled across the tracks, and vanished down a dark tunnel, like a rat racing to its hole.

2

Where

The kitchen at 7 Wolsey Road, London

Who

Wiff, Dirty George, and Nan (Maisey) King

Sounds

Kettle boiling, sizzling eggs, panting boys

"Blimey, listen to this," said Wiff, slamming himself into a chair and reading from the morning paper, the *Daily Chatter*. "TROUSERS, SKIRTS DROP ON LONDON TRAIN! British Underwear Revealed! Mystery Rabbit Takes Photo! Police Caught with Trousers Down!

"Mrs. Mustard, of East Crumpet on Thames, said she heard a strange whirring sound before her skirt fell. 'It was like some ruddy big magnet pulling everything to the floor,' said Mrs. Mustard. 'It happened so fast. One minute I was having a sip of tea; the next, I was standing in my bloomers for all the world to see.' "

"Every channel on the telly is on about it, boys," said Nan, Wiff's grandmother and chief architect of the best fried eggs on Wolsey Road. "Some nutter's invented a gadget that makes trousers fall and buttons pop."

"Blimey," said Wiff.

"Crikey," said Dirty George.

"Here are some nice eggs and chips." Nan was Wiff's only family. He remembered nothing about his parents. Nan said they died on vacation when he was just a baby. She had looked after him ever since. Nan and Wiff lived at 7 Wolsey Road in North London. At 9 Wolsey Road lived Dirty George. Wiff loved number 7's kitchen almost as much as he loved his clubhouse, Diggs. When Nan fried eggs and boiled the kettle for tea, the tiny room turned as cozy as an oven.

William (everyone called him Wiff) King was twelve years old. Wiff's best friend, George (everyone called him Dirty George) Potts was twelve, too. The boys looked like any other boys their age. Wiff had a shock of shaggy, dirty-blond hair, blue eyes, long legs, and nose freckles. A single sprig of a cowlick poked above his head. Wiff's face was open and rosy; his friend's countenance was brooding and pale. Dirty George had a thin build, long dark hair, thoughtful eyes, and a shy mouth. And like any other two boys at the end of the school year, they were giddy about the long summer days ahead.

"I've made your tea extra strong, dear."

"Ta, Nan, cheers," said Dirty George.

Dirty George elbowed Wiff.

Wiff hesitated.

Dirty George nudged him again.

"Nan, we've got something to tell you. We . . . we didn't say anything yesterday because we didn't want to worry you," said Wiff, fiddling with the tablecloth. He could invent tales for anyone but couldn't stand it if he didn't tell Nan the whole truth. "We were on the train yesterday, coming back from the zoo where we took Worm for a checkup. We stopped at Paddington Station and that *thing* went off."

"The 7:25 into Paddington Station?" asked Nan.

"Yes," said Wiff.

"On track 10?" Nan inquired.

"Yes, Nan."

"Cor," said Nan. "That's an Edison 627 diesel, built in 1938 in Sheffield. She pulls twenty-two passenger cars and five freight cars and—"

"Nan," said Wiff.

"She's seven ton and capable of seventy-seven miles per hour while—"

"NAN!"

"Oh, sorry, loves," said Nan. "You know me. Get me going on trains and I don't stop. Right. You were on the 7:25 into Paddington and something went off. Blimey! Are you all right?"

"We're okay, we're okay. We chased after the bloke who did it. He was dressed as a rabbit." Wiff proceeded to tell Nan how he and Dirty George had caught up

15

with the man and how the rabbit had threatened them. He left out the part about the knifelike teeth.

"Did you say he was dressed in a rabbit suit?" Nan's head leaned in, and Wiff noticed she was trying to absorb this particular bit of information.

"Yes, Nan, a rabbit suit," Wiff replied.

"Hmmm," she mumbled distractedly, cradling Walrus and stroking the cat as if she were intent on removing the fur. Nan straightened up, scooted Walrus to the floor, and looked both boys in the eyes. "You two will be the death of me."

"Don't worry, Nan," said Wiff. "We're the fastest runners in school."

"Yeah, like the wind," said Dirty George.

Wiff peered at Nan, wringing the dry dish towel as if she were hoping to squeeze water from it. She stepped up to the sink and finished the dishes. *I hope I haven't said something to upset her,* Wiff thought. *I'm glad I didn't mention that bloke's teeth.*

Nan's house was a railway museum. Train memorabilia covered every inch of wall. Her passion for trains began as a little girl when her father took the family on exotic journeys by rail. Her train adventures enthralled Wiff. Midnight bandits on a crossing through India. Steaming locomotives through snowy mountain passes in Austria. Going to sleep in Switzerland and waking up in Italy. Nan never tired of telling train tales, and Wiff never tired of listening.

Nan's official double-sided train station clock, which was presented to her by British Rail when she retired as an engineer, struck 7:00 a.m. Dirty George wolfed down his second helping of eggs and chips. The telly in the corner droned on with stories of eyewitnesses from the Paddington train.

Wiff dragged out a piece of rope and tied a clove hitch around the leg of the table. Tying knots helped him focus when thoughts were going off in his head like fireworks.

"Nan, I was just thinking," said Wiff. "We were the only ones to see the rabbit bloke, the guy who made that gadget. We know what he looks like."

"Go on, love," said Nan.

"Well, we could go to the police and have one of those artists draw a picture like they do in the movies and then they would make copies and send the picture to everyone and then they could catch him," said Wiff in one breath as if stopping for a pause would invite doubt.

"C'mon, Wiff, that's daft," said Dirty George. "There must be hundreds of blokes in London walking around with scruffy hair and nasty scars. Besides, I bet you he's not the one who made that gadget."

"Bet you he is," said Wiff.

"Bet you he's not," said Dirty George.

"Bet you . . ."

"Boys, boys!" Nan threw the dish towel over her shoulder and plunked down between them. "Maybe you're both right. Wiff, an artist's sketch might lead to something. And Dirty George, I agree. I don't think this rabbit bloke is the mastermind. Someone else is behind all this."

Nan stood up quickly and went to the hall closet.

She opened the door and reached in to get something. Wiff heard Nan turn a key to unlock a small metal box. He watched her stuff an envelope in her apron pocket.

"Does the newspaper say anything at all? Do they have a clue who is doing this?" asked Nan, moving abruptly to the sink, turning her back to the boys. She pulled the envelope from her apron and read the letter that was inside.

"Hang on, Nan, I'll have a look," said Wiff. He peeked over the edge of the paper and saw Nan clutching the letter. Was she shaking? He turned his attention back to the *Daily Chatter*. Under the headlines ran a full-page photo of dozens of astonished travelers in their underwear. It was the photo the rabbit took in the railway car.

"Hey! Too bad we're not in the picture!" said Dirty George, pointing to the front page.

"No one wants to see your underpants, mate," said Wiff.

"Stop larking about, you two," said Nan. "This is serious." Nan jammed the letter into the pocket of her apron and turned to the boys. Her face appeared twisted with worry.

3

What Nan Read

All in good time

Who Wrote It

Nan's brother, Basil Walter King

Is He a Good or Vile Character

Read on

Nan poured more tea. A hot cup of tea was always in reach in the King kitchen. As a matter of fact, of the 100 million cups of tea drank each day in the United Kingdom, Nan, Wiff, and Dirty George made quite a contribution to the national consumption.

"Cor, look at the time!" said Nan, springing up and gulping the last drop. "They've asked me if I want to watch while they inspect some new Kirkaldy diesels at Paddington Station this morning. They're my favorite, you know. Got to run."

Nan walked to the closet, returned the letter, and locked the box. She dropped the key in her handbag, hung her apron, and yanked on her train jacket. Before she pulled on her engineer's cap, she leaned over and gave both boys a kiss on the forehead.

"You lads finish your breakfast. I'll see you tonight." Nan stepped out the front door. "And don't get up to any mischief, you two."

"Cheerio, Nan," said Wiff.

"Cheerio, Nan," said Dirty George.

Before the sound of Nan's footsteps faded up Wolsey Road, Wiff dashed over and flung open the closet door. He grabbed the metal box and plunked it on the table.

"Oi, what are you doing, Wiff? That's Nan's!" said Dirty George.

"I know, mate. But did you see the way Nan took the letter out of the box and how she tried to hide it from us?"

"No."

"Well, I did," said Wiff. "I couldn't believe it when she finished reading. She was shaking. I thought she was going to faint."

"Lots of old people shake," said Dirty George. "My gramps had the shakes."

"I know, but Nan was definitely upset by whatever was in that letter," said Wiff. "I wonder if Nan is off to Paddington to poke around the station for clues. Maybe her story about inspecting new diesels was a bit of a dodge."

"C'mon, Wiff, you're taking this too far. You've got to trust Nan."

"I do, mate, but I wouldn't be surprised if Nan

knows more about this train business than she's letting on. That letter might be the answer. It might give us a clue why Nan seemed so upset. We need to read it," said Wiff, staring at the box as if his eyes would bore a hole into the locked safe.

"Well, how are you going to open the lock, Houdini?" asked Dirty George.

"Hmmm," said Wiff. "What would Houdini do?" Wiff picked up the box and inspected the front and back. He fiddled with the lock. "Hang on," he said.

Wiff jumped up and rummaged through a kitchen drawer. He sat down with two safety pins and tweezers. He stuck the first safety pin into the lock and held the pin firm with the tweezers. He inserted the second safety pin all the way into the lock. Wiff twisted and wiggled the pins for five minutes.

"Give up, mate, it's not going to—"

"Open?" said Wiff, popping the latch and lifting up the top of the strongbox.

"How'd you—"

"All in a book by Houdini," said Wiff.

Wiff pulled out the envelope, unfolded the letter, and read aloud:

May 1964

Maisey,

You of all people know what they have done to me. How they destroyed me and took away everything I loved. Nadia was everything to me. Boff rots in prison. I dedicated my life to Father's work and now my career lies in ruins. I've nothing left.

From the ashes of this broken man, a new life rises. Nothing can stand in my way, including you, especially you. The agony of my loss feeds my revenge. They will pay. I will crush them, I swear.

Your visit here was perilous. I'm a fugitive. Never mention me to anyone. You must never come again, or your life will be in danger. I am not the brother you knew.

Basil

"Crikey," said Dirty George. "Who's Basil?"

"He's Nan's brother. My great-uncle."

"Who's Boff?" asked Dirty George.

"Mate, I don't know," said Wiff. "I don't know why he's in prison. I don't know any of this stuff. Nan never talks about Basil. Only that some bad things happened to him and she doesn't see him anymore."

"Where's he live, then?"

"I don't know that either," said Wiff. "Hang on." Wiff picked up the envelope and checked the postmark. "Brighton. He sent it from Brighton."

"When did he send it?"

"It says May 1964," said Wiff. "That's five years ago. It's an old letter. Why is Nan reading it now?"

"Is Nadia Basil's wife?"

"I don't know," said Wiff. "Maybe."

"Could Boff be his friend? His business partner?"

"Don't know."

"And what was his father's work?" asked Dirty George, pressing Wiff like a prosecutor cross-examining a crucial witness.

"I don't know," said Wiff. "I told you. I don't know. What do you want me to do? Run after Nan and ask her?"

"Yeah, mate, that would go over well," said Dirty George. "'Er, Nan, we just happened to be reading your private letters and wondered if you could fill us in on a few names.' Wiff, think," he continued. "You must remember something Nan told you about your uncle Basil."

"She hasn't mentioned his name in years," said Wiff, staring at the letter as if it would reveal forgotten memories. A full minute passed. "There was something. . . ."

"C'mon," said Dirty George.

"It had to do with . . ." Wiff tapped his forehead as if to jiggle loose a recollection.

"C'mon!"

"I know!" said Wiff. "Nan said he was some sort of cracking-good artist or accountant . . . no, inventor. That's right, he was an inventor, and he worked for the government."

"Nice one, Wiff."

"But there was another thing she had told me about her brother that I wish I could remember. I think it was something to do with when Basil was a kid."

"Well, mate, I can't sit around here all day and wait for your brain to engage. I've got to walk me dog."

"Diggs in twenty minutes?" said Wiff.

"Diggs in twenty," mumbled Dirty George, stuffing a last piece of toast into his mouth and leaping up for the front door.

Wiff stood and switched off the television. He was glad Dirty George had left. He wanted to think. As much as Wiff loved Nan and his best friend, he sometimes needed to be alone.

He retrieved Nan's letter from the kitchen table and sat down in the old armchair beside the tall window overlooking the backyard. Walrus jumped up and plopped in Wiff's lap. The early June sun poured into the kitchen and lit up the room as if it were a greenhouse. Wiff leaned back, propped his feet on the windowsill, and gazed out the window.

Nan was clearly worried about what was in Basil's letter. I could see that. Basil said Nan's life could be in danger. But why? And why was he a fugitive? What had he done? And I don't understand why she would read it now. It's an old letter. Does Nan think the letter from Basil has some connection to what happened on the train?

Wiff's mind was baffled by these unanswerable questions. Maybe he was jumping to all the wrong conclusions. Just because Basil invented things didn't mean he invented the gadget in the railway car.

Wiff wanted fresh air. The sun was now shining squarely in his face, and for a moment, he held Basil's letter up to shade his eyes. In the light of the sun, an image took shape in the stationery. It was a watermark of a rabbit.

"Blimey, that's it!" said Wiff, springing up and sending Walrus scattering across the room. "I remember! Nan said Basil was obsessed with rabbits when he was a kid."

Wiff folded the letter, replaced it in the envelope

and carefully tucked it back into the box. He locked the box and returned it to the closet.

Wiff tore out the back door, over the mounds of dirt, and through a hole in the backyard fence. His mind was reeling. In the time it took to cross the abandoned lot to meet up with Dirty George, his mind had jelled around a tantalizing set of deductions: *Basil is an inventor; Basil loved rabbits; a guy in a rabbit suit triggered some kind of gadget on the train, causing chaos; the rabbit turns out to be nasty; Basil wants revenge on someone and sounds desperate; he even threatened Nan. Basil's got to be behind this! He must be the one that invented the thing on the train, and I bet you he's planning future havoc or worse!*

Who
Wiff and Dirty George

Why
Like salt and pepper, fish and chips,
eggs and bacon—it's Wiff and Dirty George

Where
Diggs, a clubhouse on a London rooftop

In one long, breathless speech, Wiff had convinced Dirty George that, indeed, Great-uncle Basil could be the villain behind the train melee. Yes, Dirty George agreed— the sharp-toothed rabbit and the rabbit watermark, the unzipping gadget on the train, and Wiff's recollection of Basil as an inventor, as well as Basil's written declaration of revenge—all of these seemed to add up to one thing: Basil had caused the madness on the train.

The Corporate Pig Whistle Warehouse was a three-story structure built long before London's row houses sprouted like spring weeds. The janitor of the building, Mr. Marvel, let Wiff and Dirty George build their clubhouse on the rooftop. Mr. Marvel helped them, too, hauling up weathered planks from an old shack he owned by the River Thames. Diggs was rickety quarters. When the wind blew through the windows, the boys imagined they were lashed to the mast of an old schooner. The place smelled like river and rotting boats.

The clubhouse held all of Wiff's and Dirty George's worldly assets. Wiff's treasures included his collection of marbles, bird feathers, comic books, and—his most prized possession—his display of knots glued to a piece of faded driftwood. Rope and bits of string hung from the half-dozen rafters in the little wooden shack. Piled on Dirty George's desk, shoved against a window, sat an assortment of white bones, dried leaves, and mounds of dirt. Dirty George was crackers about nature.

Wiff stepped out the door and scanned London's rooftops. Brick chimneys crowded the horizon. A flock of pigeons wheeled over Wolsey Road. If he shut his eyes, this was the scene that stuck in his head. This was home. Wiff returned and sat happily tying knot after knot, quite pleased that he had done such a magnificent, Sherlock Holmes–like job of deducing that Basil was the culprit. In this self-congratulatory air, he felt positively buoyant, and as per usual, words gushed from his mouth without the slightest thought behind them.

"I'm going," said Wiff, fiddling with a piece of rope, trying to tie a bowline with one hand. *Blimey*, he thought, *did I just say that?* As soon as the words left his mouth, he knew the idea was mad. He had no clue how he was going to find Great-uncle Basil and spy on him.

"What'd you say?" Dirty George sat on a wonky stool at a ramshackle desk sorting piles of dirt.

"I'm going," said Wiff. "I'm going to find Basil."

"You're barmy, mate, you are."

"No, really, I'm going to find my great-uncle Basil and see if he's behind all this," said Wiff with more bravado than belief.

"Wiff, don't be daft. You can't do that. First off, you don't know where he is in Brighton. And even if you found Basil, how are you going to find out what he's up to? You read the letter. He didn't want Nan to mention his name to anyone. You might get Nan in big trouble."

"Look, mate, the only family I have is Nan. Basil said her life's in danger if she tried to contact him again. I need to know what happened that would make Nan's brother say such a thing. I know Nan. She keeps things locked up inside. Something's going on between Nan and Basil, and she may be in trouble. And like it or not, this mad great-uncle of mine is part of my family."

"What can you do?"

"I don't know," said Wiff. "But it's up to me to try to do something. He's my family, isn't he? I've got to find out what he's up to."

"Are you going to tell him who you are?" asked Dirty George.

"If and when I meet Basil, I won't tell him I'm

related to Nan. I'll say I'm a neighbor. You know I'm good at lying." Wiff's voice grew passionate. His face reddened. "Who else is gonna do this?" Wiff continued breathlessly, as if by vocalizing the words he might believe them. "Nan can't. We can't get the police involved. Basil's a fugitive. I've got to do it!"

Wiff's dramatic outburst settled over Diggs. He yanked a long piece of rope from an overhead rafter.

"I've got to do it for Nan. I've got to see if I can find out what Basil's up to," said Wiff, flicking a noose over the head of a stuffed pigeon in the corner of Diggs. "And who knows, maybe I'll save England to boot."

"I don't think Basil wants to destroy England, mate."

"You don't know. Nan said he worked for the government. And in the letter he said he wants revenge. 'I will crush them,' he said. Who knows what he plans to do? It's me, mate. It's up to me to find out his plans. That letter from Basil knocks around my head like a trapped fly bashing on a windowpane."

"Wiff, you're serious."

"Of course I'm serious."

"Crikey. When are you going, then?"

"Today. Now. As soon as I pack," said Wiff.

Wiff watched Dirty George mix two piles of dirt together.

"Well, seeing as I can't trust you to save England all on your own and knowing that I can run faster than you, I should bloody well go with you."

"No you can't," said Wiff with a big grin.

"Can't what?"

"Run faster than me," said Wiff.

"Can, too."

Wiff tied a loop and chucked it over Dirty George's head.

"Thanks," said Wiff.

"For what?" replied Dirty George, yanking off the knot.

"For coming."

"Who else is going to uncover the mystery of Great-uncle Basil?" said Dirty George.

"And save England," said Wiff.

"It's up to us, right?" said Dirty George.

"Right. It's up to us."

"As long as we don't meet up with that mad rabbit from the train."

"C'mon, mate, let's go," said Wiff.

The boys grabbed their rucksacks. Wiff chucked in cans of sardines (*love sardines*), matches (*fire makes warmth*), rope (*put me on a desert island and give me only one thing, I'd want a stout piece of rope*), pencil and paper (*everyone writes rescue notes on desert islands*), a small bottle and stopper (*you've got to put the rescue note in something*), tiny torchlight (*light keeps away dark*), and sturdy rope and balls of twine (*you can never have enough*).

"You bringing Worm?"

"A bit of fresh air might cheer her up," said Dirty George.

"Worm's a she?" asked Wiff.

"Worm is a girl and a boy. But I think of her as a girl."

Dirty George dug into a jar full of leaves, moss, and dirt. Worm twirled around Dirty George's hand. He held her up to his face. Worm's mouth was an orange slice. Boy and worm examined each other.

"Who's a lovely worm, then?" said Dirty George, making squinty eyes and puckered lips. "Who wants to go for a lovely little walkies?"

Worm was a three-foot-long, Madagascan giant worm. Her natural color was brownish pink, but since pining for the jungle, she'd turned dark brown. Dirty George volunteered at the London Zoo's rainforest exhibit. The zookeepers knew Dirty George was smashing with animals. Everyone agreed he should try cheering up Worm.

Wiff listened to the morning sounds of Wolsey Road through the open windows of Diggs. He tried tying the impossible knot again.

"Bleedin' knot knummers!" he said, ditching the rope.

"Still can't tie that nasty knot, eh?"

"It's a right tricky one." Wiff stuffed the ropes in his rucksack. "I'll write Nan a short note. How much in Diggs's bank?"

Dirty George pried up a wooden floorboard and pulled out a dented metal box.

"Five pounds ten shillings," said Dirty George, counting the last penny.

"Well, I've saved nearly four pounds for some big marbles I was going to buy at Tom's Toys. We can use that," said Wiff.

"I know where my dad keeps his pub money. I can nick a few quid."

"You be careful, mate." *So Dirty George will steal some of his father's drinking money,* thought Wiff. *Less pub money, less spent on drink. It makes sense.*

"We've got about ten pounds," said Wiff. "That's

enough for two student tickets. Might even have money left over for sweets."

Wiff wrote a note to Nan. He promised he'd be home on the evening train. The boys dashed out of Diggs, sprinting across the roof like racers.

There were four ways to reach the ground from Diggs. Take the stairs—fast. Steal down the fire escape—rickety but sure. Hug the rope ladder—not easy when the wind blew. Cling to the knotted rope—even harder when the wind blew.

"C'mon," said Dirty George. "Let's do the ladder this time."

"Blimey," said Wiff. "Just because you like heights, doesn't mean everyone does."

"It's good practice. You go first."

Wiff shot Dirty George a look that could freeze water. Wiff tugged the straps on his rucksack and threw his leg over the edge of the roof. He grabbed the rope ladder and eased his full weight onto one of the rungs. He clung tight and inched down. This was always Wiff's scariest but happiest moment. He hated heights but bet his life on his knots. As he descended, he checked each knot. They looked solid and strong. Dirty George followed and met him on the ground.

The boys ran along the back of the Corporate Pig Whistle Warehouse, over the mounds of dirt in the abandoned lot, and through a hole in the fence. They emerged on Wolsey Road. While Dirty George scooted home to swipe some of his dad's pub money, Wiff ducked inside number 7. He plopped his note for Nan on the kitchen table and thought to rifle through Nan's collection of postcards. Wiff figured he might find a clue or two about where to search for Basil in Brighton. He found a lot of cards from an engineer on the Brighton train. They were marked *Timothy Thompson, engineer.* Wiff jammed the cards back into Nan's postcard box. As Wiff poured Walrus a bowl of milk, a grin worked across his face. The trail to Basil had just gone from cold to warm. Ten minutes later, he met Dirty George, and the boys struck out to search for Great-uncle Basil.

5

Combined Weight of the Wolsey Warriors
424 pounds

Combined Intelligence of the Wolsey Warriors
Equal to a rhinoceros

Two Words That Describe the Wolsey Warriors
Dull and Dangerous

"Oi, Wiff, by the way, where we going?"

"Brighton," said Wiff. "Remember Basil's letter was postmarked from Brighton. Besides, Nan loves postcards. I poked through the lot. She's got a load from someone named Timothy Thompson, an engineer on the Brighton train. Maybe we track down this bloke and see what he knows."

The Wolsey Warriors stood guard beside The Rusty Blackbird, an ancient pub and the only establishment on Wolsey Road. The Wolsey Warriors were Ian Pepper, Stu Desmond, Sid McKenzie, and Halsey Heath. Wiff saw the Warriors look up. He was on full alert when the gang crossed the street to intercept them.

"Cor, what's that smell? It smells like dirty feet," shouted Ian Pepper, the leader of the Warriors and head bully.

"Smells like nasty wet rags," said Stu Desmond.

"Naaah, it smells like bleedin' rubbish!" said Halsey Heath.

"If it isn't smelly poor Potts," said Ian. "I wonder what he's got in the rucksack, then?"

"Never mind them, Wiff, let's just keep moving."

Wiff slipped a length of rope from his back pocket and tied slipknots.

The Wolsey Warriors crowded shoulder to shoulder, blocking the pavement.

"Where we off to, boys?" wheezed Stu Desmond. "Camping? Running away from home? Although it's not much of a home now, is it, Potts? With your dirty dad and your dirty mom and your dirty little sister in rags?" Stu reached out to poke inside Dirty George's rucksack.

"Leave him," demanded Wiff.

"King, you're a marvel, you are," said Ian. "Why you messing about with this one? Blimey, how do you take the smell?"

The Warriors grabbed their noses and fanned the air.

"Hang on," said Wiff. "This calls for a prayer."

"Are you blinking daft?" said Ian. "That sounds like a bunch of weaselly rubbish."

"No, really, close your eyes and put your hands together," said Wiff. "I'll recite my new prayer for the Warriors."

"C'mon, lads," said Ian. "This will be a good one."

The Warriors did as they were told: closing their eyes, clasping their hands. Wiff looked quickly at Dirty George and nodded. Wiff whipped his rope forward, dropped the noose over Ian's clenched hands and tugged. The knot tightened.

"What the bloody hell!" Ian yelled.

Wiff tossed the other end of the loop over a nearby iron railing and yanked on the knot. Ian was trapped. Dirty George dug into his suit pocket and flung a handful of fine dirt into the astonished faces of Stu, Sid, and Halsey. The mighty Warriors bent over, cursing, spitting dirt, rubbing their eyes.

Wiff looked at Dirty George. "Run!"

"You bloody gits!" screamed Ian. "We'll get you for this!"

Where

Angel Road Railway Station

Mood

Giddy

Time of Year

Early June

Wiff and Dirty George didn't stop running until they reached the train station at the Angel.

"Did you see Halsey's face?" Wiff doubled over in fits, whacking his friend's back.

They looked back along Wolsey Road and ducked behind the red brick station. They'd ditched the Warriors.

"Right," said Wiff, trying to focus on the task at hand. "It's half past eight. Let's buy tickets and find good seats."

"Can we give Worm a bit of a stretch?" asked Dirty George. "She may want to eat."

"Yeah, sure. You walk Worm. I'll get the tickets."

Wiff returned and spied Dirty George kneeling in a coarse tangle of weeds behind the train station. He saw his friend remove Worm from the rucksack. She crawled to the ground, burying her head in the train station dirt. Dirty George dug his hands into the soil beside Worm and lifted a handful of earth to his nose. He sniffed. He stuck his tongue to the dirt and tasted. Wiff watched him take a bite and shovel the rest into his suit coat pocket. *This kid is really bonkers. Blimey, who wears his dad's hand-me-down suits every day of the year? And who eats dirt? No one. That's why I like him.*

Wiff walked up holding the tickets. "Two round-trips to Brighton. How's the dirt?"

"A bit of a smoky flavor," said Dirty George.

"Hard finding good dirt nowadays, isn't it, mate?"

The boys eyeballed Worm as she finished eating. Dirty George stuffed her back in his rucksack.

"C'mon, mate," said Wiff. "Let's go catch Britain's menace."

The boys hopped aboard and found seats in the middle of the railway car. They plopped down beside a large picture window and stared out, waiting for the train to move.

"Cor, what's that smell?" said a burly man two seats down the aisle. "It smells like the dust bin."

Dirty George sunk in his seat and shielded his face with a hand.

"It's that one over there," whined a boy sitting near the man, pointing a finger at Dirty George. "He smells like old fish."

"Naaah, it smells like Granny's false teeth," said the girl beside the boy.

The family moved their seats and opened one of the tiny windows to let in fresh air.

"Does that ever get on your nerves? People saying you smell?"

"I've gotten used to it," said Dirty George. "But sometimes I feel like hiding."

"They're just dolts," said Wiff, glaring at the boy at the other end of the railway car. "Never mind, mate. How are your parents doing, then?"

"Dad's back on the dole and lives at the pub. Mum doesn't care. Sis and I do the best we can. You're lucky. You've got Nan. I wish I could live with you and Nan."

"What if you moved into Diggs? I'd be your butler. I'd serve Nan's kippers and toast every morning."

"Smashing, Wiff. I'd love that."

"All aboard!"

The train jerked and chugged away from the station. The locomotive gathered speed. London's houses and streets gave way to meadows, hedgerows, and groves of trees. Wiff yanked two pieces of old rope from his bag. His fingers moved like the tentacles of an octopus, independent of one another. His right thumb cinched the loop while his index finger worked the line through. Wiff looked out the window while his fingers kept tying.

Dirty George dug Worm out of his rucksack.

"Is she cheering up, then?" Wiff watched Worm explore the seat cushion.

"Yeah, she's had a bit to eat. Her brown skin is turning pink. A good sign."

"Speaking of eats," said Wiff, "shall we find the grub car? I'm starving."

"You go on. I've got a bite right here." Dirty George patted his suit coat pocket. Wiff smiled and took off to find the dining car.

"Two meat pasties, please. And an orangeade, shaken, not stirred." Wiff felt very James Bondish, on his very own secret mission. He even scanned the crowd in the café car before he wolfed down the food and walked to the front of the train. He thought he'd make some inquiries. When he reached the locomotive, he saw a sign on the door: Enter at Your Own Risk—Timothy Thompson, Engineer. Wiff couldn't believe his luck. This was the very man who'd sent Nan the postcards.

Wiff knocked. No one answered. He knocked again, louder. Still no answer. He turned the knob and shoved open the heavy metal door.

The sound of the engine bashed his ears as if he'd put his head inside the funnel of a tornado. Wiff watched the engineer grip the throttle with a massive, hairy hand and lean out the window, watching the tracks.

"Helloooo!" shouted Wiff above the roar, tapping the man's shoulder.

"Oi, what you doing here?"

"I'm Wellington Potts, sir." Wiff could lie his way out of a straightjacket. "My brother and I are going to Brighton on a church project. There's a lady who looks after us. She's our neighbor. Her name is Maisey King. She loves postcards and she showed us all the ones you sent from Brighton. I remembered Maisey once said she had family in Brighton. She doesn't see them anymore. I wanted to see if I could find out anything about them."

"Cor, help us," bellowed Timothy Thompson.

"Maisey King. I haven't seen Maisey in ages. Well, listen, me old cocker, can't talk now. When we get in, I'll come and see you, and I'll set you right." The engineer turned his attention back to the tracks.

"Thanks, then!" hollered Wiff. "See ya!"

With his ears ringing, Wiff bought a postcard of a train in the buffet car and wrote another note to Nan telling her they were on a secret mission and not to worry. Wiff paid for a stamp and popped the postcard in the mail slot beside the chocolate bars and walked back to his seat. Dirty George's eyes were closed. His head leaned on the railway car window, his cheek scrunched up against the glass.

Wiff nudged his knee. Dirty George opened one eye.

"Listen, I chatted with the engineer. We're all set. He's going to point us in the right direction when we get to Brighton. Oh. I told him we're brothers and Nan's our neighbor. She looks after us. We won't tell him who Nan really is. A tiny fib, all right?"

"Jolly good." Dirty George nodded, closing his eye.

"Oh, by the way, my name is Wellington." But Dirty George was already fast asleep.

Wiff stared out the window. His hands reached for two pieces of rope—one thick, one thin—and without looking he tied a sheet bend. He untied the knot and tied it again. As the train rolled closer and closer to Brighton, Wiff tied the sheet bend 152 times before he fell asleep, wondering if finding Great-uncle Basil was turning out to be easier than he thought.

7

What Happened in 1841
London to Brighton railway completed

Best Place to Doze
On an afternoon train to the sea

Number-One Song in Great Britain in 1969
"Get Back" by the Beatles

Wiff and Dirty George were dozing soundly as the train pulled into Brighton and jolted to a stop. The passengers filed out of the cars until the train was empty. The boys rubbed their eyes, looked up, and shuddered. Timothy Thompson, all six feet six inches, leaned toward them like a predator sizing up its prey.

"There, there, boys, sorry to surprise you," said Timothy Thompson. "Beautiful city, Brighton. Lots to do. Lots to see. And, of course, you're off to find Maisey's family."

"Should we get our gear and meet you in the station?" asked Wiff.

"No, no, me old cocker," replied the engineer. "You stay put. Brighton's a big town and I need to point you in the right direction, if you're going to find Maisey's family. Give me a sec to sort out a few things and I'll have you on your way."

Wiff hadn't noticed how huge Timothy Thompson was when he first saw him leaning out the window of the engineer's cab. Here in the confines of the passenger car he looked like a gorilla. His hairy arms, as thick and taut as jungle vines, spanned the width of seats. When the muscles on his arms twitched, the snake tattoos slithered.

Wiff felt trapped. He reached for a piece of rope. Dirty George fingered loose dirt in his coat pocket.

"Sit tight, me old cockers," said Timothy Thompson, backing away, smiling. "Souvenirs from the West Sussex Railway Company." The engineer held out his arms. Dangling from the end of each pork-sausage index finger was a chain and an official train conductor's whistle.

"Ta," said the boys.

"Might come in handy. You never know. Be back in a jiff, me old cockers. Got to park me locomotive."

Timothy Thompson turned sideways to negotiate the narrow train aisle. He flung open the railway car door and then closed it shut with a thud. The noise was followed by a clang of keys, which was followed by the sound of a click.

"Nice whistle, eh, mate?" said Dirty George.

"Yeah. Brilliant."

Dirty George held Worm and blew the whistle in her face.

"Good afternoon, Wormy-worm," said Dirty George, holding Worm up to his eyes.

"Do worms hear, then?"

"Yeah, they see light and feel vibrations," said Dirty George. "So I suppose she hears this."

The train shuddered and crawled out of the station. They glanced out the window. The train switched tracks and eased into a crowded area of parked trains.

Wiff scanned the car door that Timothy Thompson had just shuffled through. The clank of keys and the noise of a click gnawed at him.

"Hang on, mate. Want to check something."

Wiff zipped down the aisle. He turned the handle on the car door. It was locked. He tugged. The door wouldn't budge. "Try the other door!" shouted Wiff.

Dirty George walked to the other end of the car and yanked on the handle. It was latched. "Bleedin' bonkers," said Dirty George. "We're prisoners!"

Who

Wiff, Dirty George, Worm,
and various train spiders and insects

Inside Temperature

70 degrees Fahrenheit;
21 degrees Celsius

Time Lapse Since Chapter 7

Exactly 11 minutes, 13 seconds

"Hey ho, me old cockers. Sorry about the lockup. Bit of a habit of mine." Timothy Thompson pushed open the railway car door.

"Blimey, you had us worried, Mr. Thompson," said Wiff.

The engineer carried a trainman's lantern and a toy trumpet. "Well, never mind that, because . . . " Timothy Thompson's voice boomed, becoming more theatrical. He fixed the light on the railway car door. He gave a blast on the trumpet. "Presenting live, in car number 5, straight from an engagement in the club car, the one and only—can you put your hands together and give a great warm welcome to—Mr. Basil King!"

The door opened, and in hopped two people wearing rabbit costumes. One held the door, while the other tossed confetti. In the lantern light, the confetti twinkled like dancing fireflies. Timothy Thompson blew another blast on the trumpet, and Basil King entered. The rabbits applauded.

Wiff and Dirty George were dumbstruck.

"Thank you, thank you, so happy to be here," said Basil King. "Oh, you're too kind."

The rabbits continued to clap.

Basil King was a tall, thin man with a face full of angles, large ears, and a sharp nose. His long hair was dyed black and matted to his head. He wore rings on every finger. His eyes sparkled like sequins. In his sky-blue tuxedo with pink lapels, he looked like a deranged nightclub performer.

"A man walked into a bar . . . ," said Basil. The rabbits burst out laughing.

"Oh, you're too kind. Why did the chicken cross the road? Because his pogo stick was at the menders!" The rabbits hopped with laughter.

"'Ello, 'ello, 'ello, what's all this?" asked Basil, turning his attention to the two boys who stood gawking in disbelief.

"Right, Mr. King," said Timothy Thompson. "Let me introduce you to Wellington Potts. He says he's a neighbor to your sister, Maisey, and he's inquiring about family she has in Brighton." The engineer turned to Dirty George. "Sorry, me old cocker, I didn't catch your name."

Dirty George cleared his throat. He might have nibbled on a bit too much soil. "George Potts. Me friends call me Dirty George."

"A giraffe walked into a pub . . . ," said Basil. The rabbits burst out laughing.

"Sooooo," said Basil, glaring at the boys. "You've come to find out about Maisey's family. Well, find me you have. So what do you want to do with me? Or perhaps the better question is, what shall I do with you? You see, my little darlings, I'm a busy man. I have an organization to run. I have a country to undermine. And here you come snooping. Dear, dear."

"Mr. King," said Wiff, standing, girding himself, willing his voice not to crack. He tried to look Basil squarely in the eye. "My brother and I are on a church project, and while we were in Brighton, we thought we might learn something about our neighbor's family. Maisey doesn't know we're here."

"What time is it when a hippo sits on a watch? Time for a new watch," said Basil. The rabbits doubled over in laughter.

Wiff couldn't believe this man was Nan's brother. He couldn't believe this man was HIS great-uncle! He was crackers.

"Soooo, my little darlings. Dear old Maisey. How is the old duck? You see, boys, life has dealt me a lousy hand. When I was your age, I was tormented. Bullies at school picked on me like a dog worries a bone. They stole my beloved rabbit and turned it into rabbit pie. A moment of silence, please, for Ben." The boys watched as everyone in the railway car bowed heads for five seconds.

Was this the reason Basil surrounded himself with rabbits? He was trying to keep alive the memory of a long-lost pet?

"My career was wrecked," Basil continued. "My family was destroyed by ruthless men and heartless governments. I've bided my time. I've planned my revenge. Guess who's laughing now."

"But," stammered Wiff. "We only—"

"Silence!" Basil screamed.

"Please," begged Dirty George.

Basil clapped his hands over the boys' mouths, silencing them. He then rammed their heads together, squashing their faces in his hands, glowering into their eyes.

"Two boys walked into a railway car," said Basil in a wicked whisper, "and were never seen again."

The rabbits snickered, slapping their sides.

"Tie them up and blindfold them." Basil bowed. The rabbits clapped.

Wiff went for his rope. Dirty George dug his hands into his pocket for dirt. But in a lightning-quick move, Timothy Thompson seized the two boys and stuffed them under his arms like sacks of laundry. The rabbits tied the boys' hands behind their backs. The last thing Wiff and Dirty George saw before they were blindfolded was Basil King waving to an imaginary audience.

Imagine

A private barge somewhere in southern England

Speed

6 knots (1 knot = 1.15 miles per hour)

Population of England

45 million

Wiff's eyelids sprang open. Everything was black. Wiff bolted upright. Then he cautiously reached out with his fingers. He moved his hands down and felt a thin mattress. *Am I on some sort of cot or bed?* He heard someone snoring nearby.

"Mate, is that you?" whispered Wiff.

"Mmmmm."

"Dirty George, wake up!"

"Crikey, I'm awake," mumbled Dirty George. "Where are we?"

"Don't know," said Wiff.

"What's that noise?"

"Sounds like running water," said Wiff.

Wiff twisted around and felt behind him. He grabbed a fistful of fabric and yanked on it. A scrap of bright sunshine penetrated the dark. Wiff blinked and recognized a round porthole. He leaned over and looked out.

"Blimey, mate," said Wiff. "We're on a boat!"

Dirty George leaped up from his berth, jammed his head beside Wiff's, and peered out the porthole.

"How'd we get on a boat?"

"Don't know," said Wiff. "The last thing I remember was Timothy Thompson dragging us out of that train. The rabbits blindfolded us, and then everything went black."

"They must have drugged us," said Dirty George.

"'Oh, what a beautiful morning! Oh, what a beautiful day!'" sang Basil.

The boys spun around as a large television flickered to life on the opposite wall. Basil's smiling face filled the screen. "Wakey, wakey, my little darlings. Time for some morning telly," said the televised Basil. "Hang on! What a naughty, naughty host I am. You're two growing lads. You must eat and drink."

No sooner had Basil finished that sentence than the sound of a key was heard in the lock. Two rabbits, carrying a tray of tea and buttered toast, opened the door to the room and switched on the cabin light.

"Meet Flopsy and Mopsy," said the televised Basil. The two rabbits bowed. "Breakfast, my little darlings, compliments of our good ship, the H.B.B. *Lapin*."

"What?" asked Wiff.

"H.B.B. *Lapin*," replied Basil. "His Basil's Barge. We may be mad hatters, but we are gracious mad hatters."

Flopsy and Mopsy set the breakfast tray on the floor, bowed, and hopped away, locking the door behind them. Wiff smothered his toast with strawberry jam. He dug a can of sardines out of his rucksack and slapped a few of the little fish on top of the jam. Dirty George sprinkled his toast with good English earth. The boys were ravenous and scarfed down the grub.

As the boys sat eating and sipping tea, they gawked at Basil on the television eating and sipping tea. The televised Basil would look up occasionally from his toast and cheerfully announce, "Bon appétit!"

When Wiff and Dirty George had finished their meal, Basil wiped his chin, folded his napkin, and said, "Right, my little darlings, now that our tummies are stuffed, I beg you to flip on the film projector and watch a fascinating program. It's brought to you by Basil Productions. The star of the show is me. Perhaps you might be persuaded to join our cause. It's fun. It's exciting. IT'S SINISTER!"

The boys looked at each other and knew the same thought was running through their brains: Basil was definitely Bonkers, with a capital *B*.

Wiff hit the "on" switch and the projector flickered to life, filling the screen on the opposite wall with Basil's homemade movie.

A classroom came into view. The camera panned across the room and halted on a tall, thin man in the corner wearing an English schoolboy outfit: short trousers, knee-length socks, tie, blazer, and cap. It was Basil. He began speaking into the camera:

"Basil King died of embarrassment on May 15, 1919. He walked into Mrs. Marigold's class trailing a ten-foot length of toilet paper from the back of his pants. It was a scorching hot day, and you know how these things go. The toilet paper got stuck. It could have happened to anyone.

"Pork Pie Martin was the first to point to Basil's toilet-paper tail. Pork Pie exploded with laughter, which got Martha Henderson roaring, which ignited the entire classroom. Basil King sank into his chair behind his desk. He looked down and saw the toilet paper. The poor boy flinched as if he'd been stung. The laughter rose around Basil like water rising in a pool. He was drowning. He buried his head on the desk and sobbed."

Wiff and Dirty George watched the classroom scene unfold. If they hadn't been prisoners, the boys might have enjoyed the sight of Basil in a school uniform, standing in a corner, as child actors played out Basil's weird past. Basil continued narrating.

"'Class! Class!' called Mrs. Marigold, returning from the office. 'What on earth is going on here?'

"'Basil came back from the loo with a tail of toilet paper!' bellowed Pork Pie, now quite red and sweaty."

Wiff and Dirty George slammed their hands over their mouths to stop sniggering. They could hear Pork Pie Martin roaring with laughter.

"'Well, that's quite enough,' said Mrs. Marigold. 'Please open to page 5 of *Geometry and Truffles*.'"

"Although quick in stopping the cruel laughter, Mrs. Marigold could do nothing about Basil's shame.

She snatched the toilet paper and threw it away. Then she put a hand on Basil's heaving shoulders.

"'It's all right, dear. It's all right.'

"But it wasn't. Not for Basil. He'd been mortally wounded. In his mind, all he heard was the maniacal laughter. All he saw were the pointing fingers.

"He didn't move when the bell rang. He didn't budge at lunchtime. And when school ended at three o'clock, Basil remained slumped over his desk. Mrs. Marigold called the office for Basil's sister, Maisey, to fetch him.

"'Bas, c'mon, let's go home.' Maisey gently encouraged him out of the chair. 'Everything's going to be okay.'

"But it wasn't. Not for Basil. He'd been teased for years. This was the final straw. As Maisey and Basil passed the schoolyard, four boys ran along beside them. 'Poopy-pants King!' 'Need Mummy to wipe your bum?' 'Don't forget your toilet paper!' "

The film concluded with Maisey and Basil, arm in arm, walking home from school under a barrage of name-calling.

Wiff and Dirty George heard the end of the film slapping the reel.

Basil's face reappeared on the television screen.

"'Man's inhumanity to man makes countless thousands mourn,' wrote the poet Robert Burns," said Basil. "The embarrassing toilet paper incident you have just witnessed was one in a long line of inhumane events in my life. A man can be subjected to cruelty for so long before he vows revenge. If you beat a dog too many times, it will bite you.

"My little darlings, have you ever been cruel or nasty to someone? Or has anyone ever been cruel or nasty to you?"

Dirty George let a screen of black hair shield his eyes. *He knew cruelty, all right,* thought Wiff. *And I'm picked on all the time because my parents are dead.*

"I could use two strapping young lads like yourselves," said Basil. "Our cause is just; our mission, noble. We want nothing more than to set things straight. You'll join us, won't you?"

"You're mad, you are," declared Wiff. "You better let us go!"

10

Species On Board

8 humans, 2 rabbits, 1 giant worm,
162 insects and spiders

The Most Ancient Egyptian Boat

A papyrus raft

Cloud Cover

Scattered cirrostratus

Wiff and Dirty George sat in stunned silence. What was Basil up to?

"So now that you have declined my gracious offer, my little darlings, it's time for the good part. See you on deck." Basil grinned.

On the other side of the door, the boys heard the sound of jangling keys. Wiff reached for a piece of rope; Dirty George grabbed a clump of dirt.

"Crikey, Wiff, I'm scared."

Flopsy and Mopsy entered and tied the boys' hands behind their backs. The rabbits led them through a narrow passageway onto a sunny deck of a river barge.

Wiff and Dirty George blinked in the bright light. The rabbits fastened the boys to the midship mast and then hopped away, disappearing down the deck to the wheelhouse.

Wiff felt the knot that Mopsy had tied. *Hmmm, a reef knot,* he thought. *Everyone knows the reef is the wrong knot to tie two young lads to a mast on a slow-moving barge in southern England. I would have told them they were using the wrong knot. But maybe not. A nice bit of play on words there, if I do say so myself.*

Wiff and Dirty George, now alone on deck, took stock of their surroundings.

The barge was narrow and long and painted yellow. It motored slowly along a river that flowed through meadows and farms and patches of woods on either side. They could see neat villages and roads in the distance.

"Can you do something about the knots?" asked Dirty George.

"I untied mine already," said Wiff.

Suddenly, the main cabin doors swung open.

Two rabbits hopped out on deck and blew toy trumpets. The noise frightened the rooks and blackbirds feeding in the fields along the bank, filling the sky above the barge with reeling, squawking birds.

Basil stepped from the main cabin wearing a British admiral's uniform, complete with black tricornered hat with white feathers, a dark blue coat with gold embroidery, blue breeches, and white stockings. Under the splendid hat Basil wore a powdered wig. From a wide black leather belt swung an ornate scabbard and sword. Two more rabbits followed carrying a silver tray draped with a silk handkerchief.

The four rabbits and Basil moved in a procession to the midship mast. The rabbits gave another blast on the toy trumpets.

Basil drew his sword. The trumpeting came to a halt.

"Ladies and gentleman, children of all ages," bellowed Basil, "and all the people of Britain, I give you . . ." The rabbits trumpeted a fanfare. " . . . The Z.E.B.R.A.!"

The rabbits hopped forward. Basil sheathed his sword and swiped away the silk handkerchief revealing a silver plastic disk about six inches in diameter and two inches thick. The bottom and sides were bright silver, but the top was clear. In the center of the disk, pulsating the color blue, was the letter Z.

"Ah," crooned Basil, "I'd like you to meet our dear Z.E.B.R.A."

Wiff guessed it was the very gadget that had created the havoc on the train. He wondered if one of the rabbits standing in front of him was the bloke with the daggerlike teeth.

"What?" said Wiff.

"The Z.E.B.R.A," replied Basil.

"Zebra?" said Wiff.

"Zebra?" said Dirty George.

"The Z-E-B-R-A," repeated Basil. "Zipper Extraction Button Removal Atom-Smasher!"

"How does it work?" asked Wiff.

"So many questions, my little darlings. In scientific

lingo, the Z.E.B.R.A. neutralizes the magnetic and gravitational pressures by altering the ion makeup in the fabric's molecules to create a force field that opposes cohesion. In plain English, me lads, this little darling makes your trousers fall down."

"Who made it?"

"How'd they make it, then?"

"My, my, we are the curious little darlings. As I'm in a jolly-good mood today, I'll fill in the blanks. Besides, you're not going anywhere. We need a couple of live subjects for some experiments we're conducting. You'll do rather nicely."

The rabbits clapped. Basil bowed. Wiff and Dirty George stole a quick peek at each other and then gaped at Basil.

"My Department of Underground Mischief makes the ZEBRAs. At DUM, I employ forty-seven brilliant physicists, chemists, and engineers in an underground bunker called Cobwebs. They make little toys for me like the ZEBRA. Together, we plan on, eh, let's say, adjusting the future."

"What do you mean *adjusting the future?*" asked Wiff.

"And I was wondering about the dirt in Cobwebs," inquired Dirty George. "Is it tasty?"

"Enough, enough, my little darlings! Enough chitchat for one day. Our rabbits are hungry for their veggies, aren't you, bunnies?"

The rabbits on deck hopped up and down in place, nodding their heads, causing their floppy ears to bounce in every direction.

"See you shortly."

Basil and his rabbits turned to leave, but then he stopped to face the boys.

"Oh, what a naughty genius I am. You haven't had a demonstration. To engage the ZEBRA, you either hold the bottom and turn the top or . . ." Basil placed the ZEBRA on a stool in front of the two boys. He reached into his pocket and took out a small device. "Or use the remote."

He pressed a button, and the ZEBRA emitted a whirring noise. Dirty George's suit buttons popped. The boys' zippers unzipped and their trousers fell down. The rabbits bounced with glee.

"Keep an eye on my smashing invention, won't you?" said Basil, turning to leave, opening and closing his naval jacket with decisive joy. "And, oh, next time, my little darlings, wear Velcro!"

11

What Time Is It

Time to abandon ship

Level of Embarrassment

High

Miles of Waterway in Great Britain

5,000

"**W**iff, this may be our only chance. We need to escape!" said Dirty George as soon as Basil and the rabbits had gone.

"Hang on, mate," said Wiff. "First things first."

Wiff, with trousers dangling at his ankles, shuffled around the ship's mast and untied the knot binding Dirty George. "Can't believe they used reef knots to tie us up. Barmy rabbits," said Wiff.

The boys tried to pull up their trousers, but the ZEBRA hummed nearby. Wiff leaned over and grabbed the device from the stool and shook it. "How do you turn this blinking thing off?"

"Here, try this," said Dirty George. He reached into his left coat pocket for a handful of fine dirt. His right pocket held more compact soil, tasty but not right for the job. He sprinkled the dirt over the ZEBRA. It worked its way down into the small openings on the top of the machine. The sucking sound faltered and then stopped. Wiff no longer felt a downward tugging force. With the ZEBRA quiet, Wiff heard the river lapping against the hull of the barge and the distant whir of the boat's motor. The boys yanked up their trousers. Wiff pocketed the ZEBRA.

"I've got an idea," said Wiff.

"Good. It better involve going overboard."

"Give me five minutes," said Wiff. "I've got to check the main cabin."

"Are you bleedin' mad!?" said Dirty George. "Basil wants to eat us alive and you want to go and have a look?"

"Five minutes, that's all I ask. We've got to find out more about Cobwebs and DUM. Then over the side, swim to shore, and run like mad. Will Worm be all right?"

"Giant Madagascans love a dip."

"Right," said Wiff. "Follow me."

Wiff and Dirty George dashed to the main cabin entrance and glued themselves to the outside wall. Over the sound of their pounding hearts, they eavesdropped on the banter coming from the galley. They crept into the narrow galley way and found three doors. On the left side, Wiff recognized the door to the room where they'd slept. The opposite door led to Basil's cabin. Wiff was sure about this because a brass sign hung on the door that read: *Basil's Cabin*. Behind the last door at the end of the galley way came Basil's terrible cackle and the raucous laughter of the rabbits. Wiff turned the doorknob, and the boys ducked inside.

The room was crammed from floor to ceiling with books, charts, globes, bird cages, fishing rods, antique daggers and swords, and springs and gears from mechanical devices. A desk occupied the center of the cabin, and behind it sliding glass doors led to an outside deck, where the boys could see the passing countryside. It was difficult to imagine that this cabin was the lair from which Basil King directed his evil empire. It looked like the floating sanctuary of a retired history professor.

"Right," whispered Wiff. "Look around."

"For what?"

"Stuff, papers, clues," replied Wiff, "anything that might tell us where Cobwebs is located or about Basil's plans."

The moment they began rifling through the documents on the desk, they heard the ship's bell clang. A voice roared over the loudspeaker, "Captain Basil! Captain Basil! Shore call from Cobwebs! Shore call from Cobwebs!"

"I'll take it in my cabin."

Wiff heard Basil's reply and his blood froze.

The boys had seconds to hide, and they knew it.

"Quick, under the desk," Wiff blurted, grabbing the strap of Dirty George's rucksack, dragging him down just as they heard the cabin door swing open. The door shut. They heard footsteps. Then Basil plopped himself into the desk chair. Basil's knee jiggled two inches from Wiff's nose.

"H.B.B. *Lapin* to Cobwebs, over," called Basil into the ship's radio transmitter.

"Dr. Façade here. Over."

"Go ahead. Over."

"Have replicated the face of her majesty and the Gold Stick in Waiting. Over."

"How do they look? Over."

"They look like her majesty and the Gold Stick in Waiting. We're finishing work on the larynx decoder apparatus. We'll have them ready for tomorrow's anniversary of Bangers and Mash Day at Kew Gardens. Over."

"Smashing. Remember the ZEBRA goes off at exactly 1400 hours, and we pinch the Queen at 1405. Excellent work, Doctor. We'll arrive shortly. Please inform your colleagues that I have captured two live specimens for their experiments. Over."

"Thank you, Captain Basil. Over."

"Over and out."

Wiff held his breath and willed Dirty George not to sneeze. Dirty George always sneezed at times like these. Basil sat still. *Why isn't he leaving?* The boys could hear him tapping a pencil on the desktop.

Beeeeep! Beeeep! Beeeep! Beeeeep! "CAPTAIN BASIL! CAPTAIN BASIL! REPORT TO THE MAIN DECK! PRISONERS ESCAPED!"

Wiff felt the cabin shudder as Basil pounded his fist on the desk. He flung the chair back, stood up, and tore out of the room.

"Time to go," said Wiff, wriggling out from under the desk. He rushed to the cabin door and latched it. Outside he heard footsteps and voices. Then Basil's fist smashed through the cabin door, barely missing Wiff's face.

"You bloody thieves!" yelled Basil.

The boys leaped over the desk, flung open the glass doors and dove into the river. Wiff heard the ear-splitting blast of the barge's horn.

The cold water took the breath away from Wiff, Dirty George, and Worm. In a half-dozen strokes the boys reached the bank and scrambled up the shore. They could see Basil pointing and the rabbits going hopping mad.

"After them!" Basil bellowed. The barge swerved to the riverbank.

The boys dashed along the shoreline and ducked into the nearby woods. Out of sight of the barge, they ran downstream, working farther and farther away from the river. The trees, mostly English oaks and beech, had grown in a narrow wedge, about one hundred feet wide, between the river and farmland. The boys came out the other side of the trees and saw ripening fields, the color of mustard.

"Crikey, no place to hide out there," panted Dirty George.

They could hear shouting coming from the direction of the barge.

"C'mon! Quick!"

They ran along the edge of the trees. Five hundred

feet ahead they could see a low hedgerow intersecting the narrow grove of trees. A massive oak tree with great boughs and in full leaf marked the corner of the farmer's field. The boys leaned against the oak to catch their breath. Ten feet from the tree, along the edge of the hedgerow, Dirty George noticed an old badger hole barely visible in the bramble.

Wiff looked up and squinted at the uppermost branches of the oak. He shuddered. "Hope you're not thinking what I think you're thinking," said Wiff.

"You go up, I go down?" replied Dirty George.

"Blimey, thanks." The boys shook hands.

Dirty George heaved off his rucksack, parted the bramble, and wriggled into the hole, feet first. Wiff watched him work his shoulders underground. He pulled his rucksack in after him.

Wiff scuffed dirt and leaves around the edges to obscure the entrance. "You all right, mate?"

"Yeah."

"If the badger comes home, pinch its bum."

"Very funny," mumbled Dirty George.

Wiff stood under the oak tree and hesitated. He felt like crawling underground with Dirty George, but stared up at the branches and worked out a route in his head. He tossed a line over a low-hanging branch. He heaved himself up to the nearest limb. The ancient oak had wide branches, evenly spaced, perfect for stopping a fall. Wiff crawled up the tree like an inch worm. He reached the leafy canopy and tied a bowline around his waist. He tied a second knot around the trunk to secure himself. He gazed off at a church steeple in the distance and for the first time thought about what he had just overheard. *Basil plans on capturing the Queen! He wants to overthrow the government and take control of the country. This is Basil's revenge. We've got to get back to London now and warn them! We've got to save England!*

Tucked high away in the branches, Wiff spied down on two rabbits.

"Where'd those little blighters go?" the first rabbit said, leaning against the oak tree.

"Gawd knows," said the second rabbit. Wiff watched the rabbit snoop through the bushes. He caught his foot in the badger hole and tripped. "Bloody badgers!"

The rabbit nearest the tree looked up and Wiff pressed himself against the tree trunk and held his breath.

"Basil will have our bleedin' throats if we don't catch 'em!" said the second rabbit.

"C'mon, then," said the first.

The rabbits took off. When all was quiet again, Wiff reached for some rope in his rucksack and tied knots. After tying a clove hitch twenty times, Wiff parted the leaves in the thick canopy and whistled down to Dirty George.

"Oi, mate. Are you there?"

"Oi, Wiff." Dirty George popped his muck-covered head from the badger hole.

"Basil's rabbits just went by," said Wiff.

"I heard them."

"Hey, mate, stay put," said Wiff. "They're bound to come back this way. I'll whistle when the coast is clear. Okay?"

"Right, then."

Wiff watched Dirty George wriggle back in his hole.

He kept his ears peeled. A slight breeze rustled the

leaves. Suddenly, a shiny black rook landed on a nearby branch. The cheeky bird looked directly at Wiff and cawed loudly.

"Shhhhh, you daft bird."

Wiff shook the branch and the rook flapped away. Was Basil crafty enough to train birds as spies? Wiff's mind drifted to the James Bond film he'd recently seen. He loved the way Bond said, "My name is Bond, James Bond." *Maybe the bird that just flew away wasn't cawing but calling out "My name is Bird, James Bird."*

Wiff heard voices and jammed his back against the oak trunk, trying to become part of the tree.

Two rabbits burst out of the woods near the tree and ran along the edge of the field in the direction of the barge.

When silence returned, Wiff blew softly into his train conductor's whistle. He untied his safety knots and stuffed the rope in his rucksack and climbed down. Dirty George was waiting, smeared from head to toe with soil and mud from the badger hole.

"How's the dirt?"

Dirty George lifted the back of his hand up to his mouth and licked. "Bit nutty," mumbled Dirty George. "Ruddy hell, Wiff, I can't believe Basil wants to nick the Queen."

"I know, mate. Can you imagine stealing the Queen? He's a madman."

"I say we run to the nearest village, ring Nan, and tell her what's going on."

"Hang on, listen to this," said Wiff. "We've got two giant bits. We've stolen the ZEBRA and we know what his plans are. But we're missing one really big bit."

"Crikey, Wiff, what's that?"

"Where Cobwebs is," said Wiff. "We heard him say that Basil will get there soon. Cobwebs has got to be around here somewhere."

"Wiff, you're not thinking of doing what I think you're thinking of doing?"

"C'mon, mate," said Wiff. "It won't take long. We follow the barge, find out where Basil's hideout is and *then* get back to London. We'll be able to tell the police everything!"

"Wiff, you're seriously crackers, you are. We'll get bleedin' caught again. He'll murder us."

"No he won't. Trust me. We'll stay out of sight, and as soon as we find Cobwebs, we'll call Nan and head back. I promise, mate."

"If I die, who's gonna look after Worm?"

"No one's going to die, you silly twit," said Wiff.

12

Amount of Dirt Eaten by Dirty George to Date

947 pounds

Amount of Sardines Eaten by Wiff to Date

1,088 pounds

Amount of Dirt Eaten by Worm to Date

3,661 pounds

The boys tightened their rucksacks and scampered along the edge of the farm field. They stayed low, keeping in the shade of the trees. Long dark shadows crept into the mustard fields in the late afternoon sun.

They hadn't gone far when they heard a noise up ahead. The boys ducked into the bushes and saw two of Basil's rabbits acting more like buffalo, snapping branches and slapping brambles.

"You horse's bum," yelled one rabbit. "Now me bleedin' ears are covered with prickles!"

"Never mind, donkey breath," said the second rabbit. "Keep your eyes open!"

Two more rabbits appeared.

"Any sign of them?" asked the first rabbit.

"Nuf-fing," said the second rabbit.

"Basil will skin us alive," said the third rabbit.

"C'mon, back to the barge, you fatheads," said the fourth rabbit. "We'll have to tell Bas—"

"Aaaa. Aaaa. Aaaa. Chooooo!"

"Oi, hang on, did you lot hear somefin'?" asked the fourth rabbit.

"Nuf-fing," said the second rabbit.

"Just the wind, monkey brains," said the first rabbit.

"More like your rotten gas," said the third rabbit.

"C'mon, you scruffy batch of furballs!" said the fourth rabbit.

The fourth rabbit boxed the ears of the third rabbit, and then they all sprinted back to the river.

"Blimey. That was close."

"Sorry about the sneeze," said Dirty George.

"Never mind, mate," said Wiff. "Those rabbits are as barmy as Basil."

"Right nutters, sounds like."

"C'mon. Let's see where they're going."

The boys tugged the straps on their rucksacks as they rushed to catch up to the rabbits. In the distance, they could hear Basil in the middle of a tirade. They crept close and crouched behind a tree and listened.

"You bucket-load of sheep droppings! You barge-load

of gull puke! You river-load of slug slime! You ocean-load of pig snot! They have my bloody ZEBRA! How on earth am I supposed to conduct Operation Switch Queen without my ZEBRA!"

Wiff patted his pocket, double-checking that the gadget was safe. He smiled; knowing that nicking the ZEBRA had thrown a major wrench in Basil's plans.

Basil ranted for five minutes. When he'd used up all his insults, he yelled to the helmsman, "Start the bloody engines and take us to Cobwebs!"

Basil turned to the search party, all floppy-eared and morose. "You lot couldn't find rubbish in a dustbin! If those little tykes go to the police, I'll murder you! Now get on your paws and run in a circle until I tell you to bleedin' stop!"

The four rabbits darted in circles on the deck.

Wiff and Dirty George muffled their laughter.

The barge met the middle of the river and picked up speed.

"How fast can a barge go?"

"Don't know, mate," said Wiff. "But let's stay out of sight and keep up."

The H.B.B. *Lapin* eased down the river. The boys kept inside the woods, hidden among dark trunks and deep shade. They plodded on steadily, always keeping Basil's barge in view. Here and there, Dirty George knelt under a particular plant and dug around the roots to pocket a handful of dirt.

"I've wanted to try bluebell soil for ages." Dirty George rolled a clump of dirt in his mouth.

"I think I'll keep to sardines. Do you ever get tired of eating dirt?"

"Nah. I tried it once when I was a baby. I loved it so much my mum fed me dirt all the time. Dirt's cheap, you know. Dad's been in and out of work and on the dole since I was a baby. Mum's done the best she could. You know, dirt's not bad when you mix it with things. But I like it plain."

"How's dirt and sardines go?"

"Smashing, Wiff. You ought to try it."

The boys tramped on into the long afternoon. Wiff tied knots and lassoed branches as they traipsed through the woods. He never missed a shot.

"Crikey, you're getting better and better with that rope."

"I want to be the best, one day," said Wiff. *And I think I can, too,* Wiff thought. *Nan says I was born to tie knots. Mum and Dad were killed by rope. All I know is that if I had been there, I might have saved them.*

The boys had traveled less than a mile when the H.B.B. *Lapin* swerved sharply left. The barge had turned off the main river into what looked like a side stream. Up ahead the land rose in narrow hills and wooded dales. The boys watched the barge move quickly away from the main river and disappear behind a line of trees.

"C'mon, quick! Let's run!" said Wiff. "We don't want to lose it!"

By the time Wiff and Dirty George reached the riverbank of the narrow channel, the woods had swallowed up the barge. There was no sight of it. No sound of the motor. No wake on the water.

The H.B.B. *Lapin* had vanished.

13

Wiff's Favorite Rope
Braided nylon

First Civilization to Make Rope
Egyptian, dating back to 4000 to 3500 BC

First Rope's Material
Water-reed fibers, flax, grass, papyrus, leather, animal hair, and date-palm fibers

Wiff and Dirty George scoured the bank like weasels. The vegetation thickened, becoming a maze of bramble and bracken. They clawed another hundred feet into the thicket. An impenetrable tangle of plants blocked their way. They could still see the channel, but it looked as if it entered a green grotto, a secret passage hidden by vines and willowy branches.

"Crikey, Wiff, this is crackers."

"C'mon, then. Turn back. We'll find another way."

They retraced their steps, eased out of their rucksacks, and pitched down in the grass.

"Wiff, I think we've lost them."

Wiff was angry with himself. *We should've kept a closer watch. We should've stayed nearer the barge. I can't believe we let Basil get away!*

"Bleedin' barge busters!"

"Hang on, Wiff. I've got an idea. Let's look about for a log we can float on or some wood we can lash together. We'll make a raft."

The boys poked about the riverside for something that would carry them down the channel.

"Crikey, Wiff, what's that?"

Wiff saw his friend pointing to the river.

Where the river and channel met sat a girl in a rowboat.

"Where'd she come from?"

"Don't know," said Dirty George. "Maybe we're seeing things."

"Don't be daft, mate. It's a girl. Looks like she's reading. She might give us a ride."

"Hellooooo!" called Wiff.

The girl waved. She put her book down and rowed toward the bank in swift, easy strokes. Wiff noticed the strength of her pull. He turned to his mate to say "Blimey" but noticed that Dirty George stood gaping at this girl in a boat. As she glided closer, Wiff gulped. Her eyes were as blue as his. A pink sunbonnet perched on a head of long blond hair. The girl wore a ball gown hiked up over her knees, revealing knee-high socks—one yellow, one purple—and orange high-top plimsoles.

"Hello. Did you see a barge come this way?"

"Long or short?" the girl asked.

"Long," said Wiff.

"White or brown?"

"Yellow, actually."

"Sorry," the girl said. "I once saw a short, white barge when I was little, and yesterday I saw a long, brown barge. But I haven't seen any long, yellow barges today."

"I'm Wiff. Here's me brother, Dirty George."

"I'm Daphne."

"Daphne, do you mind giving us a lift down this channel a bit?" said Wiff. "We were following a barge."

"The long, yellow barge?"

"We think it went down there." Wiff turned and pointed in the direction of the channel.

"Don't mind. Pop in, then."

Wiff and Dirty George chucked in their rucksacks and stepped over the gunwales of the rowboat. They sat in the stern and watched Daphne pull on the oars. There were a million questions Wiff wanted to ask. Did she live around here? Had she heard the news about the dropping trousers? But she was concentrating on her rowing. When she wasn't turning around to check her direction, she stared at Dirty George. *It's odd the way she's staring*, Wiff thought.

"You've got dark eyes," said Daphne. "Like Heathcliff in Emily Brontë's *Wuthering Heights*."

"Oh." Dirty George's face grew red.

Wiff saw how uncomfortable his friend was and changed the subject.

"Nice day," said Wiff.

"Actually," replied Daphne, looking skyward at long fingers of high thin clouds, "those are cirrostratus."

"Oh," said Wiff, not wanting to admit that he had no idea what cirrostratus clouds were.

"Daphne, have you been down this channel before?"

"Partway or all the way?"

"All the way," said Wiff.

"By myself or with another person?" asked Daphne.

"Either," said Wiff.

"I've been down this channel partway by myself, all the way by myself, and all the way with another person. But I have never been down this channel partway with another person."

"Oh." Wiff looked at Dirty George as if to say, what have we gotten ourselves into?

Daphne kept to the middle of the channel. She headed straight for a dense wall of tangled vines and leaves. The rowboat parted the vegetation and entered a tunnel. Lamps hung from the walls and lit the river with an eerie glow.

"How do you know about this place?" said Wiff. "Where are we?"

"Should I answer the first question first or the second?" said Daphne. She kept rowing, checking to navigate, and turning back to stare at Dirty George.

"It doesn't matter," said Wiff.

"Then I'll take the second question first," replied Daphne. "As to where we are, we've reached where we're supposed to be. Now to the first question. I know about this place because I've always known about this place."

Wiff was fed up with playing her game. He didn't

like the looks of this tunnel. He didn't like the look of her stare. And he really didn't like her cryptic answers to his questions.

"We want to get out of here, Daphne."

"So soon?" she said.

"Now!" Wiff stood and reached for a rope in his rucksack. Dirty George dug for a fistful of dirt. The rowboat rocked violently.

"Don't you know you're never to stand in a rowboat?" Daphne said, pulling the boat alongside a stone dock.

Wiff made a loop in the rope. If Daphne wouldn't row them back outside after he asked politely, he'd declare mutiny and take over the ship.

"I think you two better sit down." Daphne reached under her seat and aimed a loaded slingshot at Wiff. "Someone's been looking for you."

A beam of light illuminated a curtained archway. A hand appeared and drew back the curtain. Out stepped Basil dressed in a red velvet dinner jacket.

"Ah, my little darlings," crooned Basil. "I see you've met our dear Daphne."

14

What Wiff Fancied

A Mars bar and a bag of Smarties

What Dirty George Fancied

A nice bit of old oak forest dirt

What Worm Fancied

A good stretch (it was getting cramped in Dirty George's rucksack)

Faster than you can say Basil "The Bonkers" King, a bunch of Basil's bunnies bullied the boys to shore.

"Haul them to Cobwebs!" Daphne ordered.

Wiff and Dirty George struggled but were held tight by four massive rabbits. Daphne jumped out of the boat and ran into Basil's arms.

"Oh, well done, my little Daphne. I see you've caught Mr. Potts and his smelly little brother. C'mon, everyone inside!"

Basil and Daphne took the lead, turning down a

dim passageway. The rabbits hopped after them, forcing Wiff and Dirty George to hop along.

When Wiff felt he couldn't take another bounce, the rabbits stopped. The boys collapsed in a heap at the rabbits' feet. Wiff looked up and noticed they were no longer in a dim tunnel.

"Welcome to Cobwebs, boys!" Basil threw his arms open and swirled around, gesturing to his creation.

Wiff and Dirty George rose from the cold stone floor and stood in amazement. They were in a chamber carved from a hill in southern England. But it wasn't dark or dank. Lighting fixtures on the walls, in the floor, and on tables radiated a warm glow around the hall. The size of the place reminded Wiff of the old picture house in his neighborhood. Banks of electronic equipment lined one wall. Two tunnels with muted lighting disappeared off the main chamber. Wiff noticed that the far end of the chamber was unlit so he wasn't sure how far it went.

When he looked up, Wiff understood why Basil called his laboratory Cobwebs. A web of steel cables, some as thick as tree trunks, crisscrossed the ceiling of the chamber and, here and there, hung to the floor. Basil's engineers had created a hidden fortress.

The central chamber was furiously busy. Rabbits wearing white lab coats hurried to and fro. Wiff assumed these were Basil's mad scientists. More tunnels and side chambers pockmarked the walls of the central hall. The chamber echoed with a weird cacophony: the whir and hum of massive computers, the steady thrum of electronic motors, the mumblings of mad scientists, and the flop, flop, flop of rabbit feet. Long tables were covered with glass globes the size of basketballs. Each ball contained a variety of insects. One of them teemed with buzzing and crawling wasps.

When Wiff finished his inspection of Cobwebs, he looked up to see Basil glaring at him.

"I believe you have something of mine," said Basil.

"No, we don't!" protested Wiff. "You better let us go!"

Suddenly, Wiff and Dirty George were surrounded by a phalanx of rabbits. A short rabbit standing at Basil's side rushed forward. He grabbed Wiff by the shirt collar and smiled a diabolical grin. "I'll have your throats," the short rabbit swore.

Wiff shuddered. He recognized the villain's wicked teeth and bad breath.

"Edge! Put him down!" Basil demanded. "That's not how we do things, and for heaven's sake, tuck in your rabbit suit."

The short rabbit—Edge—plunked Wiff to the ground and slunk back, grumbling.

"I proclaim we put them on Express Trial," said Basil. "Set up the court, boys! I'll get my robes."

A half-dozen rabbits scurried into action, wheeling in a large desk and an imposing chair.

"All rise, all rise," sang the bailiff rabbit. "The Honorable Lord Basil W. King now presides. Order, order in the courtroom."

Basil entered, fitted with flowing black robe, white cravat, and judicial wig, and sat down.

"Bailiff," declared Basil, "what's the charge?"

"They are charged with possession of stolen property, my lord."

"And how do you two thieving tykes respond to the charge?" asked Basil.

"You're mad! We don't have anything of yours," said Wiff. "Let us go!"

"Right. Turn out their pockets, lads," said Basil. A bunch of rabbits encircled Wiff and Dirty George and patted them down. A rabbit yanked the ZEBRA from Wiff's trousers and handed it to Basil.

"Oh, look what we have here. What naughty, naughty boys you've been." Lord Basil strolled to a table lined with the glass jars full of insects. He reached into a box and wrenched on a thin plastic glove. He twisted off the wide-mouth lid of a jar filled with ferocious wasps and gently placed the ZEBRA on the bottom. The wasps swarmed on top of the disk, but none of them touched Basil's hand. Then he tightened the lid and peeled off the glove.

"It seems you've been caught with your pants down. Ladies and gentlemen of the jury, how do you declare the defendants?"

"Guilty," shouted every rabbit in the chamber.

Lord Basil stood and pronounced judgment. "In some countries they cut off your hand if you are caught stealing," Basil began.

Edge stepped forward and smiled a wicked grin, but Basil ushered him back with a snap of his fingers.

"But we are in England and shall mete out punishment in accordance with the laws of Cobwebs."

"What should we do with them, Poppy?" asked Daphne.

"Well, dear. What would you like to do with them?"

"Can we boil them, please, like the cannibals do in *Robinson Crusoe?*"

"Hmmm," mused Basil.

"We might skewer them?"

"Hmmm."

"Can we boil them and skewer them?" asked Daphne.

Wiff shifted from foot to foot. He watched Dirty George pat his rucksack. Was Worm upset with all the talk of boiling?

"Enough of this bleedin' bilge! Give 'em to me!" shouted Edge, chomping his steely pointed teeth. "I'm hungry."

"Edge! Put those ridiculous teeth away!"

"Where I come from, that's how you sort out affairs!"

"This is not some neighborhood gang. I advise you to be silent."

Edge whipped out a four-inch blade, stabbed the desk, and hurled himself from the room. Wiff stared at the knife handle swaying side to side, the point buried in the wood.

"Good man, that Edge. But a bit, dare I say, edgy. Back to you, Daphne, my dear. As you were saying, we could both boil and skewer the prisoners," said Basil. "But would it not be a better idea to observe them for a while, as we do with our jars of insects?"

"Jolly good, Poppy."

"Maybe they'll become your very own playthings, my little Daphne. But for now, throw them in the Bubbles!"

Wiff and Dirty George were snatched up and not so gingerly tucked under the arms of two very big rabbits. The rabbits walked to the opposite end of the chamber, where it was quiet and shadowy. They stopped at the foot of a large wooden platform. Out of the darkness above, the boys watched two giant glass eggs, as large as hot-air balloons, slowly descend on steel cables.

"Crikey, Wiff, what in blue blazes?"

The Bubbles touched down on a rubber pad in the center of the wooden platform.

"Behold the Bubbles, my little darlings!" exclaimed Basil over the chamber's loudspeaker. "One ton of polished glass, four inches thick, waterproof, fireproof, energy efficient, self-sustaining, climate-controlled with all the amenities of home. You should be cozy, boys. But we made them out of glass so . . ."

Basil handed the microphone to Daphne.

"We can watch you like you were bugs!"

15

Years to Build Cobwebs
7

Number of Real Cobwebs in Cobwebs
0

Why
Anti-cobweb spray developed by
Basil's Department of Underground Mischief

Wiff didn't like the look of this. A rabbit shoved him into a bubble. Etched on the glass door were the words *Bubble One*. Dirty George was heaved into Bubble Two. Wiff didn't like being separated from Dirty George. He didn't like all the talk of boiling and skewering. He didn't fancy hanging fifty feet from steel cables in a glass bubble. But most of all he didn't want to be trapped in a bubble when it was urgent to get to London.

The doors were latched, and the Bubbles slowly rose. Wiff sprawled on the floor, pressing his stomach and hands flat to the glass. He watched in terror through the bottom of the Bubble as it rose in the air. Wiff hated heights. Having nothing but a wall of glass between himself and a stone floor fifty feet below made him queasy.

The Bubbles stopped when they reached the ceiling of Cobwebs. Five minutes passed before Wiff eased off the glass floor. He noticed Dirty George moving about, checking out his Bubble. Wiff's breathing relaxed and he looked around. The floor of his Bubble was about ten feet long and seven feet wide, about the size of the kitchen at home. A round door on one wall looked to be the only way in or out. Next to the door, a heavy red drape obscured a small platform attached to the glass wall. Wiff pulled open the thick cloth and peeked in to find a small toilet and washbasin.

"Blimey," he mumbled to himself, "Basil's thought of everything. How long's he planning on keeping us here?"

He saw Dirty George banging on the wall of his Bubble. Wiff waved. Dirty George looked worried. Wiff couldn't believe he'd gotten his best friend mixed up in all of this. Wiff jiggled his head as if to shake off these troubling thoughts. But it was no use. He blamed himself.

"My little darlings." Basil's voice echoed over the chamber's speakers. "Are you settling in?"

The Bubbles slowly descended. They stopped a few inches from the ground. Basil spoke excitedly to a cluster of rabbits in lab coats. Daphne stood off to the side, swirling a rainbow-colored scarf, staring at Wiff and Dirty George.

Now Basil was dressed in full military uniform, complete with a chest of colorful medals. Wiff reckoned Basil's fake handlebar mustache stretched nine inches across his upper lip.

A rabbit unlocked each of the doors on the Bubbles as Basil continued his animated conversation.

"My ensemble is war hero," said Basil, spinning around in an exaggerated modeling pose. "What do you think?"

"Fab, Poppy," said Daphne. "You look like Sgt. Pepper!"

"Oh, jolly good. I love the Beatles."

At the mention of the Beatles, every rabbit in earshot stopped what they were doing and began singing in booming voices, "WE ALL LIVE IN A YELLOW SUBMARINE, A YELLOW SUBMARINE, A YELLOW SUBMARINE! WE . . ."

Basil raised a hand. The singing stopped. "It's my favorite song, you know. And guess what, my little darlings? My DUM is developing a yellow submarine. Won't that be fun!"

"And it will be all mine, right, Poppy?"

Wiff saw Daphne's face light up. Was she really as daft as Basil?

"Yes, yes, my dear. The yellow submarine, Cobwebs, the H.B.B. *Lapin*, my entire magnificent operation will one day be all yours."

Daphne raised her arm and pointed a finger at Wiff

and then at Dirty George. "Can they call me Queen Daphne, Poppy, like in my comic book, *Sheena, Queen of the Jungle?*"

Wiff stole a peek at Dirty George. He raised his eyebrows. Daphne *was* really as daft as Basil.

"They will, my little Daphne, if the little darlings know what's good for them."

Wiff and Dirty George leaned against the glass walls of their Bubbles.

Wiff cleared his throat.

"Ah, where are my manners?" Basil waved the boys out of their glass jars. "Boys, meet the Five Doctors," said Basil, gesturing to each rabbit. "Dr. Up, Dr. Down, Dr. Watt, Dr. Stick, and Dr. O."

The five lab-coated scientists bowed.

"Let me take a moment to describe the nature of their investigations," Basil continued. "Dr. Up conducts research in things that go up. And as you might have surmised, Dr. Down works on things that go down. Dr. Watt, like my hero, Benjamin Franklin, experiments on all things electrical. Dr. Stick researches adhesive qualities. The woman simply loves glue! Last but not least, our good Dr. O. When I think of aroma or bouquet or scent or even stench or stink, I think of Dr. O—dear Dr. Odiferous."

Wiff wondered if this was the time to try to make a dash for it. He and Dirty George could outrun anyone, but which was the way out?

"The Five Doctors have required living subjects for some time to conduct an experiment or two. So, boys, consider yourselves laboratory rats."

The Five Doctors hopped excitedly in one place, clapping paws.

"Drs. Up, Down, and Stick, help yourselves to the tall blond prisoner. Dr. Watt and Dr. O," Basil said, drawing circles with his military cane in front of Dirty George's face, "avail yourselves of this smelly little scalawag."

Wiff didn't like the look of the three doctors. Two mega-rabbits grabbed Wiff by the arms and hoisted him off the floor. With Drs. Up, Down, and Stick leading the way, they hauled him to a nearby tunnel. As the tunnel swallowed him up, he looked over his shoulder to see Dr. Watt and Dr. O strap a nasty-looking helmet with wires onto Dirty George's head.

16

Greenwich Mean Time (GMT)
20:25:51 (8:25 p.m. and 51 seconds)

Why Is GMT Mean
GMT is the mean (average) time that the earth takes to rotate from noon to noon

Number of Hours Since Boys Left Nan
36 hours

The two mega-rabbits shoved Wiff toward a chair in the corner of a crowded laboratory. They stood guard as Dr. Up, Dr. Down, and Dr. Stick bent over control boards and banks of electronic panels. Wiff went to sit but missed the chair, slid down, and sat on the floor. The rabbits grabbed Wiff under the arms and hoisted him up into the seat. He tried to think of when he had last slept and remembered it was on Basil's barge. And it wasn't a good night's sleep at that. It seemed like weeks since he'd really slept. As he watched the three weird doctors fiddling about with dials and buttons, his eyes grew heavy. His head drooped to his chest, and he was lulled into a deep sleep by the sound of a soothing electrical hum.

I'm flying over the rooftops of London. I can see Diggs. Look! There's Nan on the steps of 7 Wolsey Road. She sees me. She's waving. I can't believe I'm home. I have to land, but I don't know how. Oh no! I'm falling, falling, fall . . .

Wiff woke with a start. His heart froze. He was floating facedown in the air—like a leaf caught in a draft of wind—ten feet above the stone floor of the laboratory. His fingers tried to grasp the rope in his trousers. Could he tie himself to something? His head inched sideways. Wiff's bulging eyes fixed on Dr. Up (or was it Dr. Down?). The doctor was pointing something directly at him. *What is that thing?* he thought. *Was it a brown wing-tip shoe?*

"Oi, he just woke up," said Dr. Up.

"Good. I'll bring him down with the gravity shoe," said Dr. Down.

The scientist turned a dial on a panel that was attached to a wire that was attached to the brown shoe. Wiff felt a slight shudder and slowly descended on an elevator of air. His fingers touched the floor, followed by the full weight of his body. His heart began to beat again. The shock at waking and finding himself floating on air turned to anger.

"Are you bloody mad?!" Wiff's eyes blazed from the short doctor to the tall doctor.

"Careful, you flying lab rat," said Dr. Down. "We might elevate you to the ceiling and see what happens when we push the free-fall button."

"Oooo, it's a lovely evening for flying lessons. I'd love to get that on camera, Doctor," said Dr. Up.

Wiff gulped. The thought of them filming him smashing to the stone floor was too grisly to contemplate. These two were bonkers enough to do it.

"I'm sorry, but just no more heights. Please," Wiff begged. "I think I might be sick." Wiff looked pale. But he wasn't taking any chances. He dragged a length of rope from his pocket and slung it around his waist. If they were thinking of putting him on the ceiling, he wanted some rope nearby.

"Dr. Stick," said Dr. Down, "he's all yours."

"Thank you," said Dr. Stick, taking the shoe from Dr. Down and handing it to Wilson, her assistant. "We're going to affix the subject to a predetermined location on the ceiling—"

"Nooooo!" shouted Wiff, but his protests were drowned out.

"And the subject should not fidget." Dr. Stick turned the dial on the panel, and the gravity shoe hummed.

"Position the subject to Locus One," said Dr. Stick.

"Positioning subject to Locus One," repeated Wilson as he guided Wiff to a light-colored patch on the stone ceiling.

"Deactivate gravity shoe," commanded Dr. Stick.

"No!" screamed Wiff in a panic, scanning the ceiling for something to hold on to. "Please! No!"

"Deactivating gravity shoe," replied Wilson.

The hum from the shoe went dead. Wiff's back, arms, and legs were stuck solid to the ceiling. Petrified and helpless, staring facedown at the floor, Wiff felt like a fly caught in a web.

"Bravo! Bravo!" cried Drs. Up and Down, pointing up at Wiff and slapping Dr. Stick on the back.

"Thank you. Thank you, Doctors. I based my Super Stik substance on the physical and chemical properties of spider silk," mused Dr. Stick. "And yet, I improved on it. Super Stik comes in spray cans and squirt tubes."

"The subject is attached to the ceiling by SS540," continued Dr. Stick, glancing at Wiff and then nonchalantly turning her eyes downward to Drs. Up and Down. "It can handle weights up to 100 pounds and can—"

"I'm 107 pounds!" screamed Wiff, his voice echoing off the walls of the cave. "Get me down!"

"Well, well," cooed Dr. Stick as she switched on the gravity shoe.

Wiff felt a tug and heard a pop as he became unstuck.

"Seems as if I need to adjust the glue-carrying capacity of 540 to more than 100 pounds," said Dr. Stick as she guided Wiff from the ceiling using the gravity shoe.

Dr. Stick deactivated the shoe, and Wiff tumbled down the last seven feet like a goose shot from the sky. He hit the floor with a thud. Blood drained from his face. His muscles were as limp as cooked noodles. Wiff lay sprawled on the stone floor, shaking.

"We're done with you today," said Dr. Down. "We might have a go at your friend."

At that moment, a terrifying scream issued from a nearby tunnel. Wiff knew it was Dirty George. "Sounds as if someone's having an electrifying time," said Dr. Down, looking in the direction of the scream.

"It's *shocking*, what with the current price of energy," said Dr. Up, pausing for the puns to mature. "We should *charge* admission."

"Stop it! I'm getting all *tingly*," said Dr. Down. "Now, as to our own investigations, Doctors, I would say they were a *stunning* success."

"Yes, Doctor," said Dr. Up. "I concur."

"Me, too, Doctor," said Dr. Stick. "Basil will be very happy to add the gravity shoe and Super Stik to his DUM arsenal."

Wiff, still slumped on the stone floor, watched the doctors jotting notes and turning off machines. He glanced at the ceiling. The sight of it made him shiver. "Take him back to Bubble One," said Dr. Down.

The mega-rabbits hauled Wiff from the floor and pulled him toward the cave entrance.

"Wait!" Wiff wedged his foot into a crack in the stone floor. The rabbits jerked to a stop. He turned and faced the doctors. "Do you realize what he wants to do? Basil's going to kidnap the Queen. He wants to take over England. He's mad! We've got to stop him!"

"Ooooh, kidnap the Queen," said Dr. Up, mocking Wiff. "Take over England. Ooooh, what a naughty man."

"You're not really going to help him do this, are you?"

"Help?" pondered Dr. Down. "Let's see. To assist or aid, lend a hand, be of service."

Wiff turned red. "You're crazy!" he shouted. "You'll all go to jail!"

"Enough!" demanded Dr. Stick. "Enough! Or I'll smear your lips with Super Stik. Take him away."

"You won't get away with this!" roared Wiff. "I'll—"

A rabbit paw slammed over Wiff's mouth, stifling his outcry. The rabbits dragged him back to the Bubble, chucked him inside, and locked the door. Wiff sprang up to check on his friend. He banged on the glass walls of the Bubble and screamed, "Dirty George! Dirty George!"

Dirty George lay on his back in his Bubble. Nasty red gashes smeared the side of his head, his nose ran with blood.

17

Number of Rabbits in Cobwebs

97

Diet of 97 Rabbits

Mostly lettuce

Heads of Lettuce Needed to Feed 97 Rabbits Daily

48.5

Wiff kept banging on the glass until his fists turned raw. He fell hoarse shouting his friend's name. Dirty George didn't move. Wiff couldn't tell if he was even breathing.

Wiff watched Worm wriggle from under a pile of cushions onto Dirty George's chest. Worm squirmed under his neck, and Dirty George's eyelashes fluttered. Again Wiff hammered on the glass and shouted, giving his friend two thumbs-up. He watched his friend rub his head, rise, and stagger to the toilet. He looked as if he could use a major pile of dirt.

A wave of misery overcame Wiff at the thought of those mad doctors experimenting on his friend. Dirty George and Worm looked so helpless in that bloody glass jar. The gloominess Wiff felt at the sight of his battered friend turned to anger. *I'm going to get us out of here!*

Suddenly, both Bubbles began to descend and landed on the ground with a thump.

Wiff looked up when he heard the sound of a key in the glass door. A rabbit pushed open the door and stepped inside, carrying a tray.

"Hungry?" the rabbit mumbled.

"Starving," said Wiff.

The rabbit placed the tray on a plastic box that served as a table. Wiff lifted the lid: lettuce leaves with a side order of chopped lettuce, lettuce soup, and a glass of dark green juice squeezed from lettuce. *The whole thing looks very dodgy*, Wiff thought.

"Any fish and chips?" asked Wiff. "Or a Mars bar?"

"Sorry, mate, can't say a word," the rabbit said. "Sunday is green day. Basil wants us to have our greens today."

"I'm not a rabbit, remember?" said Wiff.

"No more talking now, mate," said the rabbit. Then, with a wink, the rabbit whispered, "I'll see what's in the kitchen."

When the rabbit turned to leave, Wiff detected a slight limp. He also noticed how the rabbit rubbed his lower back. *Maybe he's an old rabbit*, Wiff wondered.

The rabbit stopped. He rubbed his back again.

"Are you all right?" Wiff asked.

"Not supposed to talk to no prisoners," said the old rabbit. "To be honest, me back's bleedin' killing me."

"Why do you work for him, then?"

"Can't say no more," said the old rabbit. "He's been bloody good to me, 'e has, all these years."

"What's your name?"

"Can't tell you that, mate," said the old rabbit. He paused and rubbed his chin. "Oh, what's the diff. The name's Rodger."

"Hello, Rodger," said Wiff. *This rabbit seems normal, even nice,* thought Wiff.

"Sorry. Mum's the word," said Rodger. "I'll be back in a jiff to collect the tray."

Wiff stared after Rodger. The old rabbit hobbled away, pushing his cart to Bubble Two to serve Dirty George his meal. Wiff gave his friend the thumbs-up sign. He felt better. He was about to take a sip of the lettuce soup when something dawned on him.

How do farmers get rid of nuisance rabbits?

They snare them.

In a few minutes, Rodger returned to collect the dishes.

"I'm still eating," Wiff mumbled with a mouthful of greens.

"Right-o," said Rodger. "I'll be back in ten minutes." The old rabbit turned to leave.

"Eh, Rodger," blurted Wiff. "Is there any way you could bring me some chocolate? I suffer from chocoridiculitis. If I don't eat chocolate soon, I'll faint dead away."

Rodger winked and whispered, "I'll see what I can do."

Wiff studied the old rabbit shuffling to the door of the Bubble. He watched where Rodger placed his feet and how he splayed his arms to balance. The old rabbit looked down as he walked. His steps were slow and calculated. As he watched Rodger walk away, Wiff realized that, if he bent slightly at the waist, he was the exact same height as the old rabbit.

Wiff's thoughts leaped forward, unchecked, like startled cheetahs on the run. He couldn't spend another twenty-four hours in this bleedin' fishbowl and become a guinea pig for mad scientists. He had to get back to London to warn the police and save England.

Wiff banged on the wall of the Bubble, trying to get his friend's attention. Dirty George sat on the floor, sucking on a lettuce leaf. He looked up and saw Wiff hopping like a rabbit back and forth in his bubble. A moment later, Dirty George leaped to his feet and started hopping back and forth, too. The boys gave each other a thumbs-up and collapsed to the floor, laughing.

Wiff dug out his ropes and set to work. He racked his brain trying to remember how to make a rabbit snare. *I can't remember if springs are involved (I don't have any) or if I need a wire (I don't have that, either). How do I make the snare? What triggers it?*

Wiff made a mental list of the things he knew about snares. He knelt on the floor and positioned his ropes in a million different ways, but he couldn't figure out how the snare worked. He turned his rucksack upside down. Was there anything he could use for a snare? Rodger would be back any moment, and he had to come up with something quick.

In desperation, Wiff tied a poacher's noose, or slipknot. He wondered, *Would a poacher's noose work?* It had to. He quickly tied the knot and placed the large loop on the floor in front of the plastic table. He spread a white towel over the loop to conceal it. He placed pillows over the rope leading away from the knot. Rodger would need to step directly on the loop. When he did, Wiff would yank the knot tight. At least the old rabbit's feet would be tied. Then what? He didn't know.

Wiff rubbed his eyes. He wasn't sure he could do this. The old rabbit looked fragile.

What if he gets hurt? Maybe I should give it some time. We might become friends. The old rabbit might even set us free. But Wiff knew there was no time to find out.

He looked up. Rodger was unlocking the glass door. He had a chocolate bar in his paw.

18

Time of Day
Almost Bedtime

Age of Rodger, the Old Rabbit
77

Years Working for Basil
5

"Mars bar?"

"Cheers. Thanks, Rodger," said Wiff. "Eh, Rodger, you better have a look at this. The table is cracked."

Rodger limped across the glass floor toward the plastic table. Wiff stretched out on a pile of pillows. He clutched the end of the rope leading to the noose. All the old rabbit had to do now was step into the trap and . . .

"Oi, what's this?" Rodger bent to pick up the white towel in front of the table. "I'll take it to the laundry."

"No, no, please!" Wiff grabbed the old rabbit's wrist. "I had a spill. I was cleaning up the mess."

"I shouldn't be talking to you, as you know. But Basil likes to keep a tidy Bubble."

Wiff leaned back on the pillow, his hands shaking and sweaty. In the next instant, Rodger leaned over to inspect the table and stepped onto the towel. Wiff leaped up, yanking the rope high above his head. The noose snared the old rabbit's ankles. Wiff saw Rodger's eyes fill with confusion.

"Sorry, Rodger." Wiff tugged the line. Rodger's feet went out from under him, and he pitched to the floor like a fallen tree.

Wiff had spread pillows around the table so the old rabbit might land safely. But his head missed them by a few inches and hit squarely on the glass floor. The old rabbit went slack.

"Oh no! Rodger, are you all right? Blimey, what if I've killed him?"

Dreading the worst, Wiff placed his hand over the old rabbit's heart. He felt a steady *thump-thump-thump*.

Wiff looked out the Bubble. There was no one in sight. Working fast, he whipped off Rodger's rabbit mask and jammed it on his own head. He turned the old rabbit on his side and peeled away the costume, arms first, then the legs, leaving Rodger in his long underwear. The old man was curled in a ball. Wiff looked at Rodger's face. He seemed like a kind man. Wiff pushed a pillow under his head and covered him with a blanket. He tugged on the rabbit costume and, stuffing his rucksack in for a belly, zippered up. The costume fit like a charm. It came with plenty of pockets. Wiff crammed them full of rope.

Wiff checked on Dirty George. He was lying on the floor of his Bubble, playing with Worm. Outside, the central chamber was nearly dark. Wiff saw that the glass door had been left ajar with the key still in the lock. Time to play rabbit and run. Wiff dashed to the door and stepped out of the Bubble. As he did, he realized he'd made two mistakes—he left the tray behind, and he forgot to hobble like Rodger.

Wiff locked the glass door to Bubble One. There was only one key in his hand. To unlock Dirty George's Bubble, he would have to locate another key. Wiff had watched the old rabbit coming and going from one of the many dark corridors off the central chamber. The key had to be somewhere down there. Could he find the key and rescue Dirty George before Rodger woke and sounded the alarm? Could he do it before Basil or Daphne or the mad doctors discovered him missing?

The dark passageway loomed straight ahead. Wiff shuddered. He felt like a rabbit entering a fox den. He gripped the handle of Rodger's cart, trying to steady his nerves, and hobbled on, remembering to look down as he walked, just as Rodger had done. He stepped silently, pushing the trolley along the shadowy corridor, certain that the sound of his hammering heart was loud enough to wake every rabbit in Cobwebs.

19

Age When Wiff First Met Dirty George

When he was one year old

Wiff's Favorite Word

Blimey

Dirty George's Favorite Word

Crikey

"**B**limey," Wiff whispered.

From the walls of the tunnel hung portraits of Basil in various guises: Basil the lion tamer; Basil the pirate; Basil the train conductor. Little lights above the frames illuminated each portrait, casting moody shadows along the passageway. Wiff felt as if Basil's eyes were following him in the dark, and so he hobbled faster.

Up ahead, Wiff heard voices. The tunnel veered to the right and entered a well-lit circular chamber.

Wiff limped past a large wooden cabinet containing keys. Two rabbits sat at a kitchen table, drinking tea. The stone chamber had been converted into a living area with a parlor, kitchen, and a dining room. It was crammed with armchairs, TVs, stoves, and fridges. One wall of the chamber was lined with doors. One of the doors was open, and Wiff spied a bedroom with half a dozen windows draped with lacy white curtains. Beyond the windows were meadows and trees. Wiff stared and realized he wasn't looking out actual windows; they were paintings of windows with outdoor scenes. In one window, a cow looked in.

"You all right, Rodg?" asked one of the rabbits.

Wiff froze on the spot. The rabbit looked straight at him. Wiff thought of running to the cabinet and grabbing a fistful of keys. But there were hundreds hanging. How would he know the right one? First he had to get rid of the tray on the cart. And respond.

"Cold," Wiff rasped, pointing to his throat. Now he trembled. As he went to place the tray on the kitchen counter, it toppled to the floor. Clumps of cabbage and broccoli ran down Wiff's rabbit legs. Silverware and broken bits of dish covered the floor.

One of the rabbits jumped up to help. He put a hand on Wiff's shoulder. Wiff flinched. He was sweating like a boxer that had gone ten rounds.

"Poor old Rodg," said the rabbit, and bent to help. "C'mon, let's clean up this mess."

Wiff and the rabbit picked up the trash, and then the rabbit returned to the table.

"Poor old chap," said the rabbit, sipping his tea.

"He'll catch his death of cold in these bloody damp halls."

"If he ain't dead yet working all these years down here," said the second rabbit, "I don't know when he'll be."

"Suppose you're right. C'mon mate, finish your tea. Mr. Basil will have our bleedin' heads if we don't wipe down the Bubbles. He says they're a sight."

Wiff got his nerves under control. He hobbled to the wooden cabinet and swung open the glass-fronted doors. Wiff stared at the rows and rows of hooks upon which dangled countless keys. He scanned the labels, desperately trying to find the key that would unlock Dirty George's Bubble, but all he could see were bizarre names: Lettuce Loft, Bunny Boiler Room, Hare Hall, Rabbit Rumpus Room."

"Need help, Rodg?" asked one of the rabbits, placing a paw on Wiff's shoulders. Wiff clutched the sides of the cabinet to prevent his hands from shaking. He could feel beads of sweat collecting beneath the rabbit mask. Wiff let go of the cabinet, moved his head from side to side and then screwed up his shoulders. He held the key for Bubble One in one hand and made a V sign in his other hand.

"Poor blighter, can't find the key to Bubble Two," said the first rabbit, pointing to the Bubble Two key located between Bunny Boudoir and Bunny Boiler Room. "I've told Basil there are too many blinking keys in this cabinet. Ya' never find what you're lookin' for."

"Good luck, Rodg," the second rabbit said, filling his tea cup. "We'll be right along to clean that glass. Just as soon as we finish this nice cup of tea."

Wiff pocketed the key to Bubble Two and waved to the rabbits without facing them.

"Cheerio, Rodg," the first rabbit said. "Look after yourself."

Wiff limped away from the kitchen, pushing the cart. As soon as he was out of sight, he shoved the trolley out of the way and ran down the passageway until he emerged into the central chamber. Then he hobbled to Bubble Two. He could see Dirty George and Worm lying on the floor nose to nose. Wiff unlocked the door and whipped off the rabbit mask.

"Oi, mate. Want to save the Queen?"

"Crikey, Wiff. How'd you . . . ?"

"Never mind, I'll tell you later," said Wiff. "Grab your gear. We've got to get out of here now!"

Dirty George plopped Worm in his rucksack, pulled it tight, and dashed out of the Bubble. The boys scurried to the shadows of the cave wall and pressed their backs against the stones. They froze, barely breathing. Wiff slowly peeled himself from the wall and reached out to touch Dirty George's shoulder.

"You all right, mate?"

"Ready steady."

"Hold on, I'll be right back," said Wiff.

Wiff darted across the main stone hall and ducked beside the table with the glass jars of insects. When he came face-to-face with the jar of wasps guarding the ZEBRA, he gulped. *How did Basil avoid the stings when he placed the ZEBRA inside? Was he wearing a protective glove?* Wiff scanned the table for clues. He spied a box beside a terrarium full of tarantulas. It was the size of a tissue box, but instead of tissues it contained clear rubber gloves.

"Maybe, just maybe," said Wiff, tugging off his rabbit paw and wrenching on a rubber glove. Wiff spun the lid off and gently reached his hand into the neck of the jar. He could hear the buzzing and feel the vibration of wasp wings as he reached into the glass. But as his fingers closed in on the ZEBRA, the wasps quickly crawled away.

"Blimey," Wiff said, removing the disk and closing the lid. "It's like a glove made of bug spray."

Wiff shoved Basil's ZEBRA into his pocket and dashed back to the cave wall, where Dirty George was waiting. Wiff patted his pocket.

"Good one, Wiff."

"C'mon. Let's go."

"Crikey, Wiff. I think I'm gonna—"

"Oh no!"

"*Aaaa, aaa, aaa, chooooo!*"

The boys squeezed their eyes shut and held their breath as the sneeze echoed off the cavern walls.

"Sorry," whispered Dirty George. "Where to?"

Wiff spun around. He didn't know which passageway led to the outside. If they took the wrong one, they might end up facing a posse of rabbits. He looked up at a large cable. It was as thick as a telephone pole and snaked upward in wild curves and loops. The cable meshed with others and eventually formed the complex ganglion of steel cables high above. Wiff peeled off the rabbit costume and stuffed it in his rucksack.

"Up there. C'mon," said Dirty George as he pointed

to the ceiling of Cobwebs and scrambled up the nearest cable.

"We're going to climb up there?" asked Wiff, who stood with hands on his hips, not budging.

"Yeah, there's probably a way out through the roof."

"You're seriously bonkers, you are. I'm not squirming up there like a monkey, waiting for Basil and his nutters to drag us down. There must be a tunnel out of here," said Wiff, looking around.

"Oh, right. Next time I'll bring my bleedin' map of this place!"

"Look, mate, we can stand here all night and argue, but I say we try one of these tunnels."

"All right," said Dirty George, slithering down to the cave floor. "We'll do it your ruddy way this time. But if we get caught, remind me to tell you whose idea it was."

Wiff did a quick scan of the cavern. There must have been ten tunnels radiating from the main cave. "Right, we'll try this one."

They peered down the nearest passageway. It was pitch-black. Wiff reached in and touched the cold stone wall. The tunnel smelled like a mine, dank and nasty. The boys inched forward. The tunnel made a slight bend, dividing into two passageways. An oil lamp, lit by kerosene, hung on the wall, tossing flickering shadows where the tunnel divided.

"Crikey, now which way?" asked Dirty George.

"I say we go down the left one."

"I don't know. Worm and I like the look of the other

one. Right, Wormy-worms?" Dirty George held up his rucksack and spoke to Worm.

"Let's just see where this one goes," said Wiff.

Wiff led the way down the tunnel on the left. They hugged the wall, stepping like nervous deer at night, ready to bolt at the slightest noise. They had no idea of the width of the tunnel or where it led. They were creeping in the blackness, and it was eerily quiet, except for the thump of their hearts.

"Going somewhere, boys?"

Wiff and Dirty George froze.

It was Basil's voice and yet . . . it was not Basil's voice. "You sneezed before," continued the voice from the darkness ahead. "God bless you." This time the voice came from behind. It was Basil, again, but . . . still not Basil.

Suddenly, Wiff and Dirty George were caught in a blaze of light, and they shielded their eyes with their hands. They peeked through their fingers and saw Basil two feet in front of them, wearing goggles with red lenses.

The boys spun around to find another be-goggled Basil. Then a third Basil stepped out of the shadows. The boys were jammed against the cave wall surrounded by Basils, each wearing a latex Basil mask.

Still a fourth Basil marched up the stone corridor, followed by a platoon of marching rabbits.

"Ah, I see you've met my duplicates," said the newly arrived Basil, who sounded like the real Basil. "You two have become a bigger nuisance than I anticipated. You've stolen my ZEBRA for a second time. Back, please." Basil held out his hand. Wiff fished the ZEBRA out of his pants pocket and handed the gadget to Basil.

"Boys, take them to my chambers and stick them on the clock," said Basil. "I want eight guards on duty all night. I'll deal with them at 9:00 a.m. sharp, when I return in the morning. Don't let them out of your sight!"

20

Weight of Wiff
107 pounds

Weight of Dirty George
98 pounds

Weight of Worm
4 pounds

For someone who'd been electromagnetically adhered to a slowly ticking hour hand of a giant clock in a cave in southern England, Wiff slept surprisingly well.

But if he didn't scratch the itch prickling his nose in the next five minutes, he would go mad.

Of course, rubbing his nose or any other part of him was out of the question. His hands, arms, legs, and back were stuck in one position at the end of the hour hand on Basil's jumbo clock. Dirty George was stuck to the minute hand. Good thing they were both skinny, because when the hands crossed it was a tight squeeze.

"You all right, mate?" asked Wiff softly. "How'd you sleep?"

"Oddly enough, like a baby," replied Dirty George. "Only I can't feel my legs."

"No worries, mate. They've gone numb. Once we get off this bleedin' clock, you'll feel your legs again."

"Hey, Wiff?"

"Yeah?"

"You got the time?"

"Good one, mate," said Wiff, chuckling. "I think I'm on nine o'clock."

"I've just gone past twelve," said Dirty George. "It must be just after nine."

Basil burst into the chamber, dressed as the perfect World War I aviator, with leather jacket, flying goggles, and trailing silk scarf. He was smiling and flashing both hands in V for victory. A coterie of important rabbits accompanied him. They looked like important rabbits because they sported colorful sashes printed with the words *Important Rabbit*.

"Right. They're still here. Good work, lads."

Basil stepped lively about the room, picking up schedules and gadgets. Assistant rabbits buzzed around Basil, taking notes and hopping away on critical tasks. He spoke in animated tones to several of the lead rabbits. Basil was all business. Wiff watched him give some final orders, and then Basil marched up to the huge clock and faced the boys.

"Today's our big day," said Basil. "We leave for

London shortly. Before we go, however, I've decided to give you two a little taste of our genius."

On the other side of the room was a four-paneled Chinese silk screen painted with dragons. Basil turned to the screen and said, "Dr. Façade, are you ready?"

"Ladies and gentlemen, and prisoners of all ages," declared Dr. Façade, stepping from behind the screen, "I give you Her Royal Highness Queen Elizabeth and her Gold Stick in Waiting."

Wiff's jaw dropped.

Queen Elizabeth, crown and all, sauntered into the room, waving her hand. Trailing in her wake was the Queen's attendant, known as the Gold Stick in Waiting. He wore a black satin hat with a tall red feather, a black jacket with gold collar, gold epaulets, and a dozen multicolored medals pinned to his chest. A thick braid of gold dangled from shoulder to chest, and a wide blue and gold sash completed the outfit.

"Good morning, Your Majesty," said Basil, bowing his head ever so slightly. "May I introduce our two prisoners. . . . " Basil turned to the boys on the clock and asked, "And your names again?"

"Wellington P-P-P-Potts, ma'am, but everyone calls me Wiff, and me brother, Dirty George," said Wiff nervously, averting his eyes from the Queen, bowing his head. *Goodness, does Basil really know the Queen? Have I been wrong all along? Is he on the good side?*

"Mornin', you little tykes," said the Queen in a husky growl, digging a finger into an ear. "Keeping your chins up, are we?"

"My word," said Basil. "Is that you, Bunty?"

"It's me, boss," said the Queen.

"Bunty Busby, you look bloody marvelous. The Queen wished she looked so good," said Basil. "Façade, I applaud you. Your work is magnificent."

"Thank you, Basil," replied Dr. Façade. "Of course, Bunty is not wearing the larynx decoder apparatus. When he does, he will not only look like the Queen, but sound like her, too. You asked me to make you doubles of the Queen and her Gold Stick in Waiting. Here they are."

"Bravo! Bravo, Dr. Façade! Well done." Basil beamed. "A big round of applause!" Everyone clapped. Dr. Façade bowed. The Queen waved. The Gold Stick in Waiting waited motionless with gold stick in hand.

"That's wonderful," said Basil. "In ten minutes, we leave for London. I will meet you, the Queen, and the Gold Stick by my airship. . . . Oh, by the way, Your Majesty, try not to stick your finger in your ear. Doesn't look very regal."

"Right-o, boss," said the Queen.

As Dr. Façade, the Queen, and the Gold Stick in Waiting departed the chamber, Wiff watched Basil fill a leather briefcase. He spoke with his assistant rabbits, who hustled about making last-minute plans.

"You won't get away with it," said Wiff.

Basil looked up from his briefcase. "Listen, you sniveling little snot," he sneered. "You know nothing about what I will or won't get away with."

"Why are you kidnapping the Queen, then?" Wiff blurted out. Once started, he had a hard time keeping quiet.

Basil walked slowly to Wiff and stood eye to eye.

"Why am I kidnapping the Queen? WHY AM I KIDNAPPING THE RUDDY QUEEN!" Basil screamed, poking the air inches from Wiff, his face turning crimson. "Because the ruddy Queen and her corrupt cronies took everything I loved, destroyed my career, and drove me into hiding. Now we'll see who's so powerful and mighty when I bring them all down. Today is my day of retribution! No one can stop me!"

"We will." The words left Wiff's mouth before the brain could think otherwise. "Right, mate?" Wiff eyeballed his friend.

"Aaa, aaa, aaa, chooo!" Dirty George sneezed in reply.

"Ha-ha-ha-ha!" Basil doubled over laughing. "You know, you two remind me of characters in *Snow White and the Seven Dwarfs*. Everyone . . ." Basil turned and gestured first to Wiff and then to Dirty George. "Meet Dopey and Sneezy." Every rabbit in earshot clapped their paws in approval.

Basil raised his arm to silence the laughter. He stepped up to within inches of Wiff's face again and squeezed his mouth until it made a perfect O shape.

"Listen, Dopey. Your cockiness is endearing but annoying. Perhaps you derive this bravado from the closeness of your friend. Well, let's see how bold you are on your own. Me thinks you'll be less trouble if we separate you. Boys, take Sneezy down and bring him with us. Let's go. To my ship!"

A rabbit threw a switch near the base of the giant clock, and Dirty George tumbled from the minute hand. He was bundled into a canvas bag and hoisted onto the back of a massive rabbit. Basil led the way to his waiting dirigible. Wiff was left alone in Basil's chamber with the sound of the second hand pounding in his ears. The lights dimmed and Wiff trembled. His friend was gone. His itching nose was driving him mad. Their mission to save the Queen was unraveling like a poorly tied knot. Wiff was frightened and not at all as brave as Basil believed he was. He'd never felt so alone and useless. Tears crowded his eyes until he fell into an uneasy sleep.

21

Time of Day
10:00 a.m.

Hours Remaining Before the Queen Is Kidnapped
4 hours

Chance of Escaping Cobwebs and Stopping Basil
Slim

Wiff's eyes snapped open. He saw two rabbits staring at him. "What are you looking at?"

"You've been invited to tea with Miss Daphne," said one of the rabbits. The other rabbit threw the switch, and Wiff fell from the hour hand and landed with a thud. The rabbits hauled Wiff, gagged and bound, to Daphne's room. On the door hung a brass knocker in the shape of Daphne's face.

"The prisoner's here, miss," said one of the rabbits, speaking into the brass knocker.

"Come in," came Daphne's voice straight from the door knocker.

The rabbit turned the doorknob and shoved Wiff into the room. The stark, stone passageways of Cobwebs hadn't prepared him for what he beheld in Daphne's chambers. Although it was a cavernous space, the colored lights, comfy chairs, books, and clutter made the room look cozy. Three small, snug alcoves were situated off the main room. The walls were covered with psychedelic art and posters of the Beatles dressed as Sgt. Pepper's Lonely Hearts Club Band. A green carpet that looked like a lush summer lawn blanketed the bedroom floor. In one corner sat a Volkswagen Beetle decorated with daisies and peace signs.

Wiff gazed up and gasped. Floating above him were a hot-air balloon, a flying carpet, a flock of stuffed flamingos, a submarine, two flying saucers, and a yellow kite the size of a pterodactyl. Books and plastic vegetables hovered in the air, along with a blue cow, two red dogs, a Christmas tree, a set of trains, and a school of starfish. It was as if a wizard had given them wings. And above them all was a quilt of stars and flashing comets that filled the dome-shaped ceiling.

In one corner of the room, rising up from the floor and straight through the ceiling, grew an enormous tree. A cavernous stone fireplace with a crackling fire cast a rosy glow.

Wiff couldn't stop gawking at the bizarre exhibit that hovered in the air above him.

"What are you looking at?" asked Daphne, "the kite or the flamingos?"

"Gurglemean, gurglemean, gurglemean."

"What?" Daphne said. "Oh." Daphne tugged the gag from Wiff's mouth. "Say again, please."

"The submarine, actually," said Wiff.

"What's wrong with the kite and flamingos?"

"Er, nothing," said Wiff, shuffling his feet, not quite sure how to talk to this girl. "I was just looking."

"'My soul is in the sky,' you know. That's what Shakespeare wrote in *A Midsummer Night's Dream*," said Daphne, staring up with Wiff. "I think everything should float. Don't you?"

"Er, yeah, sure," replied Wiff, not quite sure what he was sure about.

"Where's the other one?" asked Daphne to the two brutish bunnies gripping Wiff. "The one with the dark hair."

"He's gone with Basil," said one of the rabbits.

"Pity. Please untie my guest. I've got my slingshot quite handy, if he tries anything," said Daphne, patting a leather holster strapped around her waist. "You two can hop along now."

"Right, miss," said the rabbits, doing an about-face and hopping out of the room.

Wiff finally had a good look at Daphne. She was tall and strapping with long arms, a freckled face, blond hair, and blue eyes. She had a wide nose like Wiff's. She was wearing tie-dyed overalls, a yellow scarf, and green plimsoles.

"You can sit down, you know." Daphne tapped the

back of a chair beside the table set for tea. She sat and poured two cups.

"I don't particularly feel like socializing," said Wiff as he watched Daphne smear butter and strawberry jam on the most delicious-looking bun he'd ever seen. He looked away. He was ravenous. His stomach grumbled.

"Someone's a bit peckish." Daphne fixed a second bun with butter and jam. She put it on a plate beside the cup of tea for her guest. Wiff stood with arms folded, not budging, eyes fixed on the floor.

"C'mon, silly," said Daphne. "Don't be cross."

"Don't be cross!" Wiff shouted. "You keep us prisoner in glass bubbles, you feed us lettuce, your great Basil sticks us to a bleedin' clock, we're surrounded by mad rabbits, and now you've kidnapped my mate! If Basil or his rabbits hurts Dirty George, I'll . . . I'll . . ."

"Thought you'd said he was your brother, then."

"He was. He is. I don't know," said Wiff, frustrated by his own lie. He plunked himself down and took a whacking-great bite of the breakfast bun. Jam dribbled down his chin.

"He's quite nice, whoever he is," said Daphne, dabbing the corner of her mouth with a napkin to indicate the jam trickling at the edge of Wiff's own chin. He got the message and wiped the jam off with his sleeve.

Wiff filled the awkward silence with eating. He dug into his rucksack and broke open his last tin of sardines. He asked for more tea. He took another bun. He looked around the table and ate until the food was gone.

"Would you like to see my bug collection?" said Daphne. "I've got a rhinoceros beetle."

"Blimey, are you bonkers?" said Wiff, pushing away from the table and standing up. "You think this is all a big bloody game, don't you, Daphne?"

"No, keeping beetles is a serious hobby of mine."

"Don't be daft. You know what I'm talking about," said Wiff, pacing back and forth across her room.

"I love games," replied Daphne, setting down her teacup and looking up at Wiff. "Now I've got to guess what you're talking about, right? Let's see. I know it's not my beetle collection. Hmmm. My hanging display?"

"C'mon, Daphne," said Wiff. "You know. This underground hideout, Basil's gang of mad scientists, a load of dressed-up rabbits. You don't find all that crackers?"

"My poppy's a genius and a very kind man."

"He's bloody mad!"

Daphne bounded up and, in one fluid motion, loaded a large marble in the elastic strap of her slingshot and pulled it taut. She took aim at Wiff's head. "Take it back. Take it back, Wiff, or I'll brain you." Daphne glowered.

"Fine. I take it back, but do YOU think it's right that Basil kidnaps the Queen?"

"My poppy knows the Queen."

"Blimey, Daphne, that's not the point!" cried Wiff. "Do you know he's flying to London at this very moment to kidnap her? He wants to ruin National Bangers and Mash Day. Besides, he's pinched my mate."

"I'm sure Poppy wouldn't hurt the Queen. He'd be in lots of trouble, then." Wiff watched a shadow of gloom pass over Daphne's face.

At that very moment, it dawned on him that Daphne would want to prevent anything bad happening to her beloved poppy. "Daphne, you have to understand that Basil is in grave danger. He could get arrested. He could get killed!"

"You're lying, Wiff."

"Go and ask one of your rabbits, then, if you don't believe me."

"That's exactly what I'm going to do." Daphne walked to the wall and tugged on a braided velvet cord that hung from the ceiling. It engaged a remote two-way radio.

"Yes, Miss Daphne? Over," said a rabbit through Daphne's sound system.

"Maxwell, can you please tell me where my poppy is and when he's planning on returning? Over."

"Basil left for London on a confidential mission, miss. His ETA back at Cobwebs is 1900. Over."

"Did Poppy leave me any messages? Over."

"No, miss. I'm sorry. Just that his mission was highly confidential. Over."

"Thank you, Maxwell. Over and out." Daphne slumped in her chair, propping her elbows on the table and making a V out of her hands in which she cradled her chin.

"Daphne, I've got an idea," said Wiff, seizing the moment. "I know where and when Basil plans to strike. If you can get us out of here, I'll lead us there, and we can stop him."

"You really are daft, you know, Wiff. You're not going anywhere."

"Daphne, listen to me," said Wiff. "You can talk

Basil out of this. You're the only one he listens to. You can convince him that this plan of his is nothing but madness."

"How do you know what Poppy is planning?"

"Because I overhead Basil talking about his plan on the barge."

"Why should I trust you?" Daphne asked.

"Look. We don't have much time. We've got to try to stop Basil from doing something really balmy. You need me, Daphne. You know you do. We need each other at the moment. You want to protect Basil, you want to keep him out of prison, and I want to rescue my friend and save dear old England."

Daphne shifted in her chair. Wiff could tell she was considering the offer.

"No. I can't!" Daphne cried out, standing up and crossing her arms. "Poppy will clobber me if I let you go. And I'm supposed to stay here and be the boss."

"Your poppy is about to do the worst thing in his life and only you can save him," pleaded Wiff, standing and facing Daphne. "And you better do it soon!"

Daphne hugged herself and groaned.

"We go on one condition." Daphne loaded her slingshot and pulled it taut. She aimed at Wiff. "You promise me you won't say a word to the police about Poppy's hideout and what goes on here."

"I promise. I promise," said Wiff.

"Poppy's identity must remain hidden," insisted Daphne. "He's all I have, Wiff. If anything happens to him, I'll lock you in the Bubble forever!"

"Trust me, Daphne. I don't mean to harm Basil."

Wiff recognized the fire burning in Daphne's eyes. She'd do anything for Basil. *I feel the same way about Nan.* "I know how you feel," said Wiff. "By the way, Daphne, if we're going to work together, I was wondering—er, I was wondering if you could stop pointing that blinking slingshot at me."

Daphne released the tension on her slingshot. She stepped away from the table. She jammed the slingshot into her holster and some marbles and a bar of chocolate into a rucksack.

"What time does Poppy plan to . . . ?" Daphne asked, looking away.

"The ZEBRA goes off at two o'clock this afternoon. Five minutes later, Basil and the rabbits kidnap the Queen." Wiff studied Daphne's face, not sure if she was taking it all in. "We've got to hurry."

"Where are we going, exactly?" she asked.

"When I'm free and we're on our way, I'll tell you."

"What happened to trusting each other?" asked Daphne.

"First, get us out of Cobwebs," said Wiff.

22

Daphne's Favorite Color
All colors

Daphne's Favorite Food
All sweets

Daphne's Perfect Day

Wake up at 10:00, breakfast on crumpets and tea in bed listening to a live string quartet, practice slingshot, practice bow and arrow, swim in river, read a chapter in her favorite book (Pride and Prejudice by Jane Austen), watch her favorite movie (Casablanca) while noshing chocolate macaroons, go for a ride on her favorite flying machine, observe clouds, practice fencing, drink tea with Poppy in the sunset tree house, walk in the woods, munch on fish and chips while touring Brighton on the top of an open double-decker bus, stargaze, sip tea, nibble on cake, and read in bed until sleep comes

Daphne hoisted her rucksack, walked to the tree trunk in the corner of her bedroom, and pressed a knot on the bark. The trunk opened, revealing a hidden lift. Daphne stepped in and turned to Wiff.

"You coming?"

"Er, yeah." Wiff stepped into the lift.

Daphne touched a button marked Treetops and up they went. Wiff wondered if Daphne was setting a trap. He fingered the rope in his pocket. *Where is she taking me? Can I trust her? This has got to be a trap. She's made escaping Cobwebs too easy.*

The lift came to a stop, but Daphne kept her finger on the "close door" button.

"Remember, Wiff," said Daphne, "I'm doing this for one reason—to make sure that nothing happens to my poppy."

Daphne released the button and the lift opened onto a round, sunny platform high in the canopy of the forest. Wiff gasped. He stepped out and looked around to see if rabbits were ready to spring. He kept his back to the tree trunk. If Daphne thought about pushing him off the edge, he'd be ready.

Daphne walked to a spot on the plastic platform and tapped her toes in an odd pattern as if she were punching in numbers to unlock a safe. The moment she stopped, half the platform slid away and a deck rose from below with four of the strangest contraptions Wiff had ever seen.

"Let's go." Daphne stepped up to the nearest machine. It resembled an open-air, two-seat, giant insect. She swung her bag in the back and hopped into the front seat. "We'll take Dragonfly."

"Daphne, where are we and what are these things?" asked Wiff, treading lightly over the transparent floor of the platform, ready to bolt at the first sign of trouble.

"This is Tree Port and these are flying machines. Poppy likes Wasp because it's the fastest." Daphne pointed to a sleek, gleaming rocket-shaped contraption. "Those are Bugs," she said, referring to two squat VW Beetle–like vehicles. "I prefer the Dragonfly. More control, better view, does fifty miles per hour with a good wind. Hop in."

Wiff climbed in beside Daphne but turned completely around to make sure they were alone and not being followed. He wondered if there wasn't an easier way to leave Cobwebs. *Do we have to fly? I hate heights!* He yanked his seatbelt tight until he thought his chest would pop.

Daphne pressed the ignition switch and Dragonfly trembled. She donned aviator goggles, a leather flying hat, and a white scarf. *Blimey*, Wiff thought, *she's wearing the same outfit as Basil.* Daphne flicked a button on the forward control panel, and Dragonfly rocked as the buglike wings fluttered and beat.

"Hang on!" shouted Daphne over the roar of the engine.

Dragonfly lifted off the landing pad, rose out of the canopy, and went straight up into the southern English air. The machine hung there suspended, its wings flickering in the summer sun. Wiff heard a steady buzz from the blades.

"Which way, then?" asked Daphne.

"Kew Gardens," gasped Wiff, pale-faced and frozen with fear, clinging to the front dashboard. "But, Daphne, couldn't we walk or take the train?"

"Buck up, mate. You'll love flying. Right, Kew Gardens," said Daphne, typing on a keypad beside her throttle stick. "I've set the navigation system, but I've flown there tons of times. Takes about 2 hours and 25 minutes if we don't run into wind. Or birds. And we're off!"

Wiff gulped.

Daphne nudged the throttle. Wiff clutched the dashboard as Dragonfly surged forward. He dared not look over the side but concentrated on staring straight ahead. He couldn't believe he was doing this. As the countryside changed below, a realization took hold of him: he'd actually escaped Cobwebs. His thoughts turned to Daphne and what she was doing. Flying!

He was gobsmacked.

"Daphne, how do you know how to do this?" called Wiff over the wind in his face, his mind boggled with what he'd seen and heard in the past few hours. "How'd you learn to fly? How old are you? Do you go to school? Where are your mum and dad? Why do you live with Basil, anyway?" A torrent of questions poured from Wiff. Daphne confounded him. Was she brilliant or slightly crackers? Wiff stared at Daphne with her dark goggles, white scarf tucked in a knot around her neck, and blond hair streaming in the wind. She looked like Amelia Earhart.

"You asked six questions. Which one shall I answer first?"

"Oh, pleeeeease," said Wiff. "Don't start that again!"

"My mum's missing. No one knows where she is. My dad's in prison."

"Blimey. What he do?"

"Don't know. Poppy won't tell me, but it was

something very bad. I've lived with Poppy my whole life. Do you have nice parents, then?"

"They're dead. Died when I was young," said Wiff. "I live with me nan in London."

"I feel like my parents are dead, too. Poppy raised me; he's my only family. He taught me to fly. I go to school in Switzerland, but I'm on holiday now. I'm twelve. How old are you, then, Wiff?"

"Twelve."

"And George?" asked Daphne.

"He likes to be called Dirty George, by the way," said Wiff. "And he's twelve, too."

"Look!" Daphne pointed below. "There's the train to London."

Wiff watched Daphne steer Dragonfly downward to the level of the train windows. She came alongside and waved to some children in their seats. Wiff tapped Daphne on the shoulder and pointed to trees looming ahead. Daphne took Dragonfly into a steep climb and leveled off.

"Wow," Wiff exclaimed. "You're good at this."

"I've spent the past two summers flying over Europe. I love Dragonfly. You know it's powered by solar cells?"

Wiff spun in his seat and looked at the dozen dinner-sized silver plates pressed into the fiberglass tail of the machine. Just then, a cumulus cloud blotted out the sun.

"Don't worry," Daphne chuckled. "We've got backup battery power."

"Bloody brilliant."

"Oh, you should see some of the inventions my poppy is working on."

"I don't get it, Daphne," said Wiff. "If Basil and his scientists can invent all these amazing things, why would he want to do something as bad as kidnap the Queen?"

"You have it all wrong, Wiff," she said. "I just know it. My poppy would never do something like that."

"If I'm wrong, why are we flying to Kew Gardens?"

"Look," said Daphne, "I know you don't like him because he stuck you in the Bubble, but he's the most amazing person I've ever known. I wish you could see what I see."

"What I see I don't like," said Wiff.

"Well, then, we're on opposite sides," said Daphne.

"Then we're on opposite sides," said Wiff.

Daphne and Wiff sat in cold silence. After what seemed like hours, Daphne broke the tension.

"What's the plan, then?" she asked.

"I don't know," replied Wiff, pulling out some rope and tying a clove hitch around a bar inside the cockpit. "Let's see what we're up against once we get there."

"Oh, brilliant, Wiff. We'll march into a royal celebration and say, 'Excuse me, we're here to save the Queen'?"

"Blimey, Daphne, I don't have all the ruddy answers, do I?" said Wiff, tightening a knot as if it were around Daphne's throat. "I know Basil plans to use the look-alikes of the Queen and Gold Stick. Somehow we've got to get close enough to figure out who's who."

"Wiff, I'll say it again. You have to promise me," said Daphne as she reached out and clutched Wiff's arm. "You won't tell a soul about my poppy."

Wiff looked up from his knot tying and into Daphne's face. He saw anguish in her eyes, as if losing

Basil would break her heart.

"Look, Daphne. I'm going to stop Basil and rescue Dirty George. But I won't say a word about Basil to the authorities. You've got my promise." Wiff didn't know if that would make Daphne happy, but she let go of his arm, and very quietly he heard her say "Okay."

Wiff looked down and noticed the landscape beginning to change.

"We're getting nearer to London," Daphne said. "Twenty minutes to Kew Gardens."

Wiff looked at his watch.

"Hurry Daphne! Time's running out!"

23

Most Clichéd Phrase in English Language
"Time's running out"

What Is Kew Gardens
One of the great botanical gardens of the world

Size of Kew Gardens
300 acres

They could spot the ceremony a mile away. A large section of lawn was covered by massive white tents topped by flapping Union Jacks and colorful pennants. They could see crowds of people. "Look!" said Daphne. "The ceremony is in front of the Temperate House."

Daphne kept well away from the site, hugging the tree canopy. She steered Dragonfly in a wide circle and flew up the River Thames to a small forest a half mile away.

"We'll land down there," said Daphne. She pointed to a grassy knoll beside a clump of trees and scattered barns and outbuildings. Wiff tugged on his seatbelt. Daphne took Dragonfly into a gradual dive and hovered momentarily before she gently touched down in the shadow of a massive beech tree. "Welcome to Kew."

Daphne and Wiff gathered up their rucksacks and dashed in the direction of Temperate House, the largest botanical glasshouse in the world. Daphne kept pace with Wiff as they ran from tree to tree. *Blimey, she's a gazelle. She can run as fast as Dirty George and I can.*

Daphne charged ahead and led them to a cluster of sheds, stables, and barns. Tractors, wheelbarrows, and gardening tools of every kind were strewn about the buildings. This was the behind-the-scenes at Kew Gardens. Stone driveways and dirt paths guided the way to the public gardens.

"The celebration is down that lane." Daphne pointed to the widest road on the other side of a clearing. "Let's keep to the side of these buildings and get down there."

They scampered alongside a row of neat outbuildings, hugging the shade and shadows. They paused for breath at the corner of a tool shed.

"Look!" Wiff pointed to a man dressed in a white dinner jacket fastening the padlock on the door of a small barn. They pressed their backs against the shed and froze. The man in the dinner jacket tugged on the lock and pocketed the key. He reached inside his jacket, pulled out a piece of paper and unfurled it. He studied the paper for a moment, jammed it back in his pocket, and ambled away from the barn.

They watched him disappear around the corner of the building.

"That's blinking bizarre," whispered Wiff.

"Very," said Daphne. "You don't wear brown shoes with a white dinner jacket."

"Blimey, Daphne, I'm talking about someone dressed like that locking up a barn. A bit suspicious, if you ask me."

"Oh, right," Daphne acknowledged.

"I think the bloke's gone," said Wiff. "Let's go have a look."

Daphne and Wiff sprinted across to the barn and pressed up against the wall. Wiff edged over to a grimy window and stood on tiptoes to peek in.

"Daphne, look!" cried Wiff.

Wiff and Daphne stretched to their full height to spy into the barn window. They could see Dirty George, bound and gagged, slumped in a chair, his head flopped to his chest.

"Gotcha!" A hand clamped over Wiff's mouth, and his arm was wrenched backward. The towering hulk of the man dressed in the white dinner jacket plucked Wiff from the ground, held him in an excruciatingly painful armlock, and smothered his scream.

"Hello, Miss Daphne," said the dashing lug. "What are you doing here with this little runaway?"

"Oh, Pablo, it's you," said Daphne. "I'm 'er. We're 'er . . ." Daphne hesitated one second more and, in a lightning-quick move, loaded her slingshot and fired a grape-sized marble at Pablo's shin.

"Ouch!" Pablo let go of Wiff and bent down, wincing

at the pain. Daphne reloaded and nailed Pablo's other shin. Pablo slumped to the ground, and Wiff whipped a bowline around Pablo's chest and arms. Wiff tugged on the knot with all his strength as Pablo rolled in the dirt. Wiff chucked Daphne a small nylon cord, and she tied Pablo's feet.

"Daphne, what you playing at? Wait till Bas—" Pablo's words were stifled as Wiff, racing as though he were in a calf-tying contest, jammed a rope across Pablo's mouth and knotted the line behind his head.

Daphne and Wiff stood over the writhing oaf.

"Stop wriggling, Pablo," said Daphne. "You'll ruin your jacket."

Wiff kicked Pablo in the shin. "That's for the armlock," Wiff said, "and kidnapping my friend."

"Enough, Wiff, let's go!"

Wiff shoved his hand into Pablo's jacket pocket and grabbed the key and piece of paper. Daphne and Wiff bolted for the barn door and unlocked the padlock. They flung open the door and ran to Dirty George.

"Blimey, mate, wake up." Wiff leaned over and shook his friend. Daphne snatched the gag away and loosened the ropes.

"Crikey, Wiff!" cried Dirty George as he opened his eyes. "You've come. I knew you would!" He slapped Wiff on the back. "Oh, hello, Daphne, what are you doing here?" Dirty George added shyly.

Daphne looked into Dirty George's eyes and brushed the hair from her forehead.

Wiff saw Dirty George turn crimson. He hoisted him to his feet and guided him to the barn door. "Long story, mate. But, you see, we're in a bit of a rush," said Wiff.

"Right. Sorry," said Dirty George. "What's the plan?"

"We've got to stop Basil. And time is running out."

"I heard Basil say the fake Queen and Gold Stick will sneak into someplace called the Rose Room," said Dirty George.

"It's the Rose-Cutting Shed," said Daphne breathlessly. "It's behind the Temperate House. I took a tour once."

"Then what?" asked Wiff.

"Dunno," said Dirty George. "That's all I know."

"Blimey, I wish we had more information," said Wiff.

"Look at the paper Pablo was reading," said Daphne. "It might tell us something."

"Good idea." Wiff dug out the paper and spread it out on the ground. "Blimey, what is this?"

The sheet of white paper was the size of a placemat. Wiff traced a single dark line with his finger. It began on the bottom left corner and swirled around a white background until it ended in the upper right. X's and funny numbers and bizarre words were sprinkled along the black line. Scrawled at the top of the page, in letters an inch high, were these indecipherable words: *s'olbaP paM*.

"It must be in some sort of code," said Wiff.

"Look's like gibberish to me," said Dirty George.

"This is no bloody good," grumbled Wiff, kicking the paper into the weeds and searching the horizon for a clue as to what to do next.

Daphne stooped and picked up the paper. She

turned it upside down. She held it up to the sun. She squinted.

"You silly boys," mused Daphne. "This is Pablo's Map. See?" Daphne pointed to the obscure title at the top of the page. "The letters are backward. The numbers are in military time. And you see this spot here marked by an X?"

The lads leaned in and stared at a gobbledygook of words: *hcniP neeuQ ta 5041 ta etarepmeT esuoH.*

"It says 'Pinch Queen at 1405'—that's five minutes after two o'clock—'at Temperate House,' " said Daphne, looking up from the paper as if she'd just read troubling news about a dear friend. "Oh, Poppy, I hope you're not going to do something very naughty." Daphne stared wistfully in the direction of the Temperate House.

"Blimey. We've gotta go. Daphne, lead the way!" shouted Wiff as the three of them hurtled out of the barn toward the celebration.

24

What Basil Was Doing at the Moment

Drinking a nice cup of tea

What Nan Was Doing at the Moment

Drinking a nice cup of tea

What the Queen Was Doing at the Moment

Drinking a nice cup of tea

If you'd watched them from a distance, you would have been hard-pressed to say who ran the fastest. They moved like winged creatures, barely touching the earth. They reached the Rose-Cutting Shed at the same time, stretching out their arms as if to grasp the first-place ribbon in a race. Without hesitation, they opened the door to the small greenhouse and found Bunty masquerading as the Queen, hiking up the royal under-garments. Beside her—or him—amid fragrant English roses, the Gold Stick in Waiting struggled to yank on shiny black boots.

Wiff, Dirty George, and Daphne attacked like wasps disturbed at the nest. Daphne dinged the Queen and Gold Stick repeatedly with well-aimed marbles, while Dirty George hurled fistfuls of loose dirt from the potted plants into their astonished faces. Wiff bonked Bunty and his sidekick with an antique watering can. They hit the greenhouse floor like felled trees.

"Uh-oh," said Daphne as the three of them stood over the comatose Queen and the Gold Stick. "Poppy's not going to like this."

"Daphne, you can't have second thoughts now. We've got to get cracking," said Wiff, already peeling away the Queen's latex mask from Bunty's face. "Right, who wants to be the Queen?"

"I love dressing up. I'll be Her Majesty," Daphne said, whipping off the Queen's undergarments from Bunty's hairy legs.

"Good," said Wiff. "I'll be the Gold Stick."

"Why you?" Dirty George picked up the Gold Stick's gold stick and gave it a twirl.

"Because you need to find the ZEBRA and chuck some dirt in it so the bloody thing doesn't go off." Wiff yanked on the Gold Stick's mask and buttoned up his jacket. "How do I look?"

"A right twit." Dirty George laughed.

"No, I think a nice twit, Dirty George," said Daphne.

It was the first time she had heard herself say his name. Her breath caught.

"You two are hilarious," said Wiff. "We don't have much time before the Queen begins her speech. Sneak through the crowd and see if you can find that ZEBRA. It's out there somewhere. All right, mate?"

"I'll try," said Dirty George.

"Good job," said Wiff, clapping him on the shoulder.

"Well, I'll be off, then," said Dirty George. "See ya', Wiff. See ya', Daphne."

"Cheers, mate," said Wiff.

"'Bye, Dirty George," said Daphne, holding out her hand.

Dirty George took her hand in his and looked at it for just a moment. It was the first time he'd ever touched a girl.

"You're hand is so soft," he said quietly.

"Well, I am the Queen, you know," said Daphne.

Dirty George turned a shade deeper than the English roses and quickly departed.

"Come on, come on!" shouted Wiff. "We've no time to lose!"

Wiff hiked up his pants and planted his gold stick on the greenhouse floor. His fake face felt rubbery and hot. In that instant, he realized the absurdity of their situation. Impersonating Her Royal Highness, Queen Elizabeth II, and her bodyguard, Daphne and Wiff were about to step in front of one of the largest ceremonial gatherings England had ever witnessed. But he looked at Daphne's face and beheld such a sense of resoluteness behind Daphne's eyes, it erased any self-doubt. They would walk onto that stage and see what happened. The rest would take care of itself.

"Remember our bargain, Wiff," said Daphne.

"Not a word about Basil. I promise," said Wiff, opening the door of the rose shed. "After you, me lady."

"Wiff," said Daphne, pausing for one last second. "This is mad, you know"

"I know," said Wiff. "Let's go!"

25

How Many Pages Until End of Story
19

What Part of The Book Have You Reached
The Climax

Will Wiff, Dirty George, and Daphne Save the Day
Read on

Wiff puffed out his chest and stepped forward.

"There's the royal tent," said Daphne, ducking into the shade of the three-story, Victorian glass building known as the Temperate House. Wiff was glad Daphne was by his side.

A round, white tent with a domed roof had been erected at the back of the Temperate House. A large Union Jack fluttered from the peak, and the coat of arms of the royal family decorated the rear tent flap. Wiff and Daphne could hear the swell of the crowd gathered on the opposite side of the building. Someone at the microphone droned on—occasionally interrupted by polite applause—about the love Great Britain showed for the monarchy, as well as for bangers and mash.

"I bet they are about to introduce the Queen," said Wiff. "C'mon!"

They stole up to the tent and Wiff peeked in. Wiff couldn't believe their luck, because luck was about the only thing going for them.

"Blimey, it's her," Wiff whispered. "She's in there sitting on a couch with the Gold Stick in Waiting. It's just the two of them."

"Well, let's get cracking," said Daphne, wrenching up the rear flap and marching into the tent. Before Wiff could formulate a plan or take a breath, he was standing in front of the Queen of England.

During the tortuous path that led to this moment, Wiff hadn't given one thought about what he would say or do when he faced Her Majesty the Queen. How could he convince Her Royal Highness that she was in danger and keep Basil's identity a secret?

Fortunately for Wiff, the Queen saved him the trouble.

She took one look at Daphne, her carbon copy, and fainted. To be honest, she let out a tiny squeak. Her eyes fluttered, her breath jolted, and her royal noggin fell into the lap of the Gold Stick in Waiting. The Gold Stick in Waiting wasn't a young man and was averse to surprises. So when the Queen's head hit his gold-embellished lap, sending her crown rolling, he, too, went woozy and swooned on top of his most royal liege. They looked like regal ragdolls crumpled on a satin couch.

"Daphne, quick, let's latch the flaps shut," said Wiff, whipping three pieces of twine from his Gold Stick pocket. While Daphne held the flaps taut, Wiff fastened the back of the tent.

"I never even got to say hello," said Daphne, wistfully staring down at the comatose monarch. "How long are you out when you faint?"

"I've no idea," said Wiff. "What's this?" Wiff reached down and pried a small folded piece of paper from the Queen's fingers. "It's her speech. You're going to need this." Wiff handed the paper to Daphne.

"Thanks."

"You might also need this," said Wiff, bending down and lifting up the Queen's crown. Wiff placed the crown on Daphne's head and bowed deeply.

"It's too big," said Daphne.

"Sorry, Your Majesty, but it will have to do," said Wiff, ushering Daphne to the front of the tent. "That's our cue." They could hear the crowd applauding as the master of ceremonies introduced the Queen. "I'll tie off this flap. That should hold them for a while. I'll be right behind you."

Wiff held open the front flap, and Daphne walked out of the tent and through the Temperate House. When she stepped onto the red-carpeted portico overlooking the sweeping summer grounds of Kew Gardens, a thunderous applause rose up. Wiff, having secured the tent with his most baffling knots, joined the Queen at her side. Trumpets blared. Wiff and Daphne stood frozen, staring at the throng of people. Both were dumbstruck. Wiff had no idea what to do next. As his eyes moved across the front of the crowd, he picked out Dirty George, who was making a slight hand gesture.

"Blimey, that's right," whispered Wiff into Her Majesty's ear. "You're supposed to wave."

Daphne nodded and her crown went flying. Wiff snatched it in the air and plunked it back on the Queen's head.

"Sorry, Mum," said Wiff. "Give them your little wave, but be careful of your crown."

Daphne raised one hand and gave the royal wave. The applause swelled. Wiff stared at Daphne. He couldn't believe it. She was into this. He looked out on a sea of people waving flags. He saw television cameras and the press corps. Dignitaries—the lord mayor, the royal family, members of Parliament—crowded the front rows. The pageantry was overwhelming.

If only Nan could see me now. Hang on. Nan loves the royal family. She's probably watching the telly right now. Blimey! Wiff looked into one of the TV cameras and waved.

The crowd hushed as Daphne inched ahead in a slow promenade to the microphone at the main podium, clutching the Queen's speech. She opened her mouth to speak and managed to only say, "Good after—" when a number of things happened simultaneously.

Wiff later tried to recall the actual sequence of events. *Did the lord mayor's trousers fall first, or was Prince Charles bonked on the head by a misguided roll of toilet paper?*

He concluded it was impossible to tell. It was as though he were watching a gigantic pinball machine gone out of control. Dozens and dozens of toilet rolls arced through the sky, and streamers of toilet paper slowly descended on the crowd. At the same time, trousers dropped, buttons popped, and Wiff saw Dirty George running frantically back and forth searching for the ZEBRA.

In the middle of the melee came a momentary hush. Audience members that were not struggling to keep their trousers up were pointing at the stage. Wiff spun around. The real Queen and Gold Stick in Waiting had woken and joined them onstage. And now the Queen was rising into the air like a helium balloon. The real Gold Stick grabbed the royal ankles and hung on.

The Queen waved feebly and uttered a befuddled "Help! Help!"

The sky above the stage had filled with Basil's aircraft. Ten or more hot-air balloons, each shaped like a rabbit's head, bobbed in the sky. Directly above the Queen hovered Basil's dirigible. It looked like a great orange carrot with a propeller and wings. Basil was leaning out of the cabin and pointing the gravity shoe directly at Her Majesty.

Suddenly, the audience broke out in applause. Wiff turned to see people smiling and clapping. He couldn't believe it! They thought this was part of the celebration.

"Wiff! Do something!" Daphne cried.

Wiff whirled around to see the Gold Stick in Waiting's hands slip from the Queen's ankles, sending the Gold Stick tumbling to the stage. Wiff had seconds to save Her Majesty. He whipped a line of rope from his pocket and flung a slipknot at the Queen's feet. It missed and whacked her on the backside.

"Goodness gracious!" squealed the Queen.

Wiff gathered up his line again, adjusted the loop, and leaned back to toss it one last time. The Queen, slowly rising in the air, was almost out of range.

"Steady, Wiff, you can do it," said Daphne, rushing to his side.

Wiff focused on the Queen's pink high heels. He uncoiled the rope and pitched the knot skyward. The loop flew up, spiraled perfectly around the Queen's feet, and pinched snug. Wiff knew he could not fight the pull of the gravity shoe, so he quickly bent down to tie the other end of the line to the metal handrail along the stage. He tugged the knot tight. The line was secure. The Queen safely hovered ten feet in the air, still smiling and waving to the crowd.

Wiff turned and looked into the faces of Daphne and Dirty George.

Taking the boys' hands in hers, Daphne kissed each of them on the cheek. "Bravo, Wiff," said Daphne. "And Dirty George, I hope I see you again."

"Where are you going?" asked Dirty George.

"Home."

Daphne stepped into the beam of the gravity shoe and began to rise.

Wiff and Dirty George grabbed hold of her hands.

"It's okay," said Daphne. "You can let go."

"But what will Basil do when he finds out it's you and not the Queen?" said Wiff.

"He'll go bonkers," said Dirty George. "Stay with us. Please!"

"Don't worry," said Daphne. "I know my Poppy. I'll tell him I did it all for him. He'll go nutters for a bit, but then he'll be smashing."

Wiff and Dirty George released Daphne's hands. She rose steadily into the air. Soon she was face-to-face with the Queen.

"Hello, Your Majesty," said Daphne. "I believe this belongs to you." Daphne lifted the crown off her head and placed it on the Queen.

"Why, thank you, I think, Your, er, er, Majesty," said the Queen.

Wiff and Dirty George watched Daphne rise higher and higher.

"Like I said, Wiff," shouted Daphne, "'my soul is in the sky'!"

The police and members of the royal family had come to the Queen's aid and were hauling her down. Before Daphne disappeared into the belly of Basil's carrot, she gave Wiff and Dirty George a quick thumbs-up. Wiff caught a final look at a red-faced Basil, shaking his fist.

With Daphne the Queen safely inside, the flock of hot-air balloons spewed billows of orange smoke. Wiff watched Basil's airship veer skyward before the fog of orange engulfed the ceremonial grounds.

"Run!" shouted Wiff to Dirty George. It took Wiff less than the better part of a second to realize he didn't want to be standing onstage with the Queen and her Gold Stick in Waiting, members of the royal family, and the Queen's security detail when the fog cleared. It would reveal the wreckage of Britain's biggest ceremony, and all eyes would be on him and Dirty George.

The boys dashed through the Temperate House and around the royal tent and sped across the grounds to the trees. They hid behind a small garden shed.

"Anyone chasing us?" wheezed Dirty George.

"No, I think we lost them in the smoke," said Wiff, stripping off the uniform of the Gold Stick and shoving it in his rucksack.

"Oi, Wiff, I finally found it," said Dirty George, yanking out the ZEBRA from his jacket. "It was under a dustbin."

"Brilliant, mate. Hang on to it."

The boys checked the area once more and then tore through the woods like leaping gazelles. They ran along the banks of the Thames and passed the grassy knoll where Daphne had landed the Dragonfly. It was gone. *Blimey, Basil thinks of everything,* Wiff thought. *He's already had it flown away. He planned every step in his great scheme to kidnap the Queen. The cloud of orange smoke to hide his getaway was brilliant. But it allowed us to escape, too. He didn't count on that. And he didn't count on Daphne helping us. We won. He lost.*

Wiff and Dirty George ran in the direction of London, triumphantly bounding along the River Thames. They had rescued the Queen and saved good old England.

26

Nan's Favorite Train
1952 Kirkaldy diesel

Level of Danger
Lessening

Desire for Home
Growing

"**A**ngel Road! Last call for Angel Road!"

"Blimey, mate!" Wiff bolted upright. "It's our stop!"

Wiff jumped up and shook Dirty George. They'd fallen asleep and the passengers in the crowded car gave a wide berth to the two disheveled boys slogging to the exit.

A half hour after the lads had leaped from the stage at Kew Gardens, they emerged from the Angel Road Railway Station. The boys yawned and stretched, watching the train leave. They set off walking to Wolsey Road.

"Crikey," said Dirty George. "There were times I didn't think we'd ever see London again."

"Well, we better keep out of sight for a while," said Wiff. "I was wearing the Gold Stick mask, but the police may have seen you, mate."

"Yeah, Wiff, Scotland Yard could be on the lookout for me," said Dirty George, spinning around to check if they were being followed. "I don't want to go to prison."

"Don't worry. I think we escaped before they got a good look at you. Basil's smoke saved us."

"Hey, Wiff?"

"What?"

"Let's send Basil a thank-you card," said Dirty George.

"Good one, mate."

The boys turned up Wolsey Road, where the Wolsey Warriors were lounging about the doorstep of The Rusty Blackbird. The gang looked slouchy but alert, like hungry lions beside a baobab tree.

"Oh, great, they've seen us," said Dirty George. "Our welcome home committee."

"Blimey," said Wiff, feeling drained and weary. "I'm in no mood for them."

The Warriors crossed the street and built a barricade of bodies.

"Oi, where've you boys been?" chortled Ian Pepper. "We have a little business to conclude with you two."

"You're the git that chucked dirt in my face!" sneered Halsey Heath, grabbing Dirty George by the collar.

"Lay off him, Halsey," warned Wiff, "or this time we'll give you a dirt sandwich."

"You think you're funny, don't you, King," said Stu

Desmond. "Well, it's time for a little payback."

Sid McKenzie grabbed Wiff's left arm and wrenched it behind his back.

"Now who's laughing?" said Ian Pepper. "We've made up a little song for you. C'mon lads."

The Warriors leaned in and cleared their throats. "Wiffy-woo, done a poo, halfway up the lamppost," they sang in unison. "Saw a ghost eating toast, ran right home to dumpy Potts!"

"You better let him go," said Dirty George, "or you'll be sorry."

"Oh, we'll be sorry, will we?" mocked Halsey Heath. "Well, you're next, you dirty—"

Dirty George thrust the ZEBRA into the air. At once, the trousers of the Wolsey Warriors fell like a stage curtain on the final act. The mighty Warriors stood like wilted stalks, staring at Halsey Heath's ratty underpants.

"Run!" shouted Wiff.

They dodged the Warriors and raced up the street.

"We'll get you, you bloody swine!" yelled Ian Pepper. The Warriors, hitching up their trousers, gave chase.

Dirty George tossed the ZEBRA to Wiff.

"Nice one, mate!" said Wiff.

The boys outran the Warriors and dashed up the stone steps of 7 Wolsey Road. They burst through the front door and slammed it shut behind them. They slumped against the back of the door, their chests heaving for breath, their voices sputtering with laughter, their hearts hammering and happy.

27

Time Elapsed Since Leaving Home
Just over 2 days

What Time Is It, Really
Time for a nice cup of tea

Is the End Really the End
It's the beginning

Wiff dashed down the hall and burst into the kitchen.

"Nan!" he shouted, and flew into Nan's outstretched arms. Wiff buried his face in Nan's chest and felt her heart singing in his ears. He breathed in smells of Pears soap and train engines and fried tomatoes and sweet tea. He hugged her so long that Nan motioned to the waiting Dirty George to come up and join the hug.

"You two are nothing but bones," said Nan, squeezing them. "Let me look at'ches."

Nan wrenched them away from her and held them at arm's length. She clasped them again. Walrus snaked between six feet and six legs.

"You lot need a good fill-up," she said. "And, if you don't mind me saying, you both reek. When was the last time you saw a bar of soap?" She maneuvered them to the kitchen chairs. They took off their rucksacks and chucked them to the kitchen floor and sat. She stood between them, holding their hands, looking at them. "Couldn't you find any soap and water in Brighton?"

Wiff bolted upright. "Nan, you knew where we were?"

"What are you on about?" said Nan. "Of course I knew where you were. When I got your postcard of the Brighton train, a lovely Smithy diesel, by the way, built in 1944 and designed to—"

"Nan!" Wiff said, clutching her arm, bringing her back to the conversation at hand.

"Sorry, loves," said Nan. "When I got your postcard, and you going on about a secret mission, I was worried to death about what you might stumble into."

Wiff stole a quick look at Dirty George. "Nan," said Wiff, "Basil kidnapped us!"

Nan's fingers clutched the boys' hands.

"Nan, listen." Wiff took a deep breath as if he were about to dive underwater. "I'm sorry to have to tell you this, but when we got to Brighton, Timothy Thompson, the engineer, locked us in the train car. Then mad Uncle Basil came with people dressed in rabbit costumes, and they were all laughing and joking and—"

"Blowing in toy trumpets," piped in Dirty George.

"And Thompson grabbed us, and the rabbits must have drugged us and—"

"To think I once fancied that bloke," said Nan, shaking her head.

Three cups of tea later, Nan had heard the whole story.

Wiff and Dirty George slumped back on the kitchen floor. They were spent. They'd told Nan as much as they could remember. Nan, perched at the edge of her seat the entire time of the boys' tale, now eased back into her chair. She looked at the ceiling, slowly shaking her head from side to side, and then stared straight at Wiff and then at Dirty George.

"Nan," said Wiff, "all I want to know is why's Uncle Basil doing this? Why did he want to kidnap the Queen?"

"I don't have all the answers, dear, but you two deserve the truth. You've been through enough, that's for sure. It's my turn to tell you a story. Pop the kettle on, love," Nan said to Dirty George. "Let's have a cup, and I'll put you in the picture.

"I don't know how much you learned about your great-uncle Basil, but things are not what they seem. Wiff, you asked about why he's doing these things. This might explain."

Nan dug a letter from her apron pocket. It was Basil's letter, the one Wiff had taken from the strongbox. Nan read it aloud.

Snatches of the letter resonated in Wiff's head.

"*. . . they destroyed me and took away everything I loved.*"
"*Nadia was everything to me.*" "*Boff rots in prison.*" "*. . . my career lies in ruins.*" "*I've nothing left.*"

"*They will pay. I will crush them . . .*"

"*. . . never come again, or your life will be in danger.*"

"Basil sent this letter five years ago," Nan said, gazing at it with eyes that were far away. "You've got to understand, loves, Nadia is . . . Nadia was Basil's wife. Boff is their son." Nan paused. She placed the letter in her lap and looked at Wiff and Dirty George.

"I'm going to tell you things that must stay in this room. Do you both swear?"

"Yes, Nan," said Wiff. "I swear."

"I swear," said Dirty George.

"I kept many things from you, love," said Nan, taking Wiff's hand and holding it in her lap. "Please don't hate me, Wiff. I thought it was for the best."

"Nan, don't be silly. I could never hate you," said Wiff.

"My father, Walter King," Nan began, "your great-granddad, Wiff, started Britain's secret service, MI5. Basil went to work as an MI5 agent when he was twenty-four years old."

"Uncle Basil is a spy!" Wiff interjected.

"He was. He worked in the gadget department. Within a few years, he headed up the department and was soon providing advanced security gadgets to the Queen and her family. Basil loved his career, helping to protect England. He loved carrying on the tradition of our dad.

"At the peak of his career, when traveling for the service, he met and fell in love with a Russian intelligence officer named Nadia Balalaika. Fraternizing with enemy agents was strictly forbidden. But love has no borders. Basil and Nadia kept their marriage a secret. Then Nadia became pregnant and gave birth to a son named Boffery. They called him Boff for short."

Wiff yanked two worn lengths of rope from his rucksack and tied loop knots. The water in the kettle boiled over, but no one budged.

"Despite his secret marriage, Basil's life was as full as he could have hoped. He became the personal adviser of security measures to Her Majesty. But Basil was the 'boss's son,' and there were those on the lower rungs of MI5 who were determined to bring Basil down.

"During one of their secret rendezvous, Basil and Nadia were photographed by someone at MI5, and the pictures were sent anonymously to Moscow. When the KGB learned Nadia was married to an enemy agent, she was imprisoned. Basil was bereft. Boff was determined to save his mother. He risked everything by attempting to steal the jewels of the Russian Imperial Court on display at the Tower of London. He hoped to bargain with the Russians for his mother's release. The biggest tragedy was that Boff was foiled by the very antitheft measures that his father had developed. Boff was found guilty and sent to prison. Shortly thereafter, Basil's secret marriage to a Russian spy was made public, and he was unjustly accused of masterminding the theft of the Russian jewels with his son. The day the police came to arrest him, Basil fled. He turned into a master of disguise.

"Wiff, you asked why Basil's doing this. All I know is that everything he loved—his wife, his son, his career, his country—was stolen from him. He was broken and bitter.

"The last time I met Basil was in Brighton, shortly before I received his letter. I pleaded with him to seek legal help to clear his name and gain the release of his son. But Basil was determined to strike back, to bring down the very power and authority that destroyed his life."

"But, Nan," asked Dirty George, "where is Basil's son now?"

"Still in jail, love, and will be for a very, very long time, I'm afraid."

"What's happened to Nadia?" asked Wiff.

"I don't know. It's been many years now. I couldn't say if she is alive or—"

"Why the rabbit costumes?" asked Dirty George.

"Basil loved bunnies when he was a boy. He kept them as pets. There was one rabbit that he particularly adored. But school bullies stole Basil's rabbit and gave it to the cook at the King's Head Pub. Made a lovely rabbit pie, he did, with wild mushrooms and a lovely Stilton cheese."

Nan stuffed Basil's letter into her apron and looked up at the railway clock over the sink. "Do you know it's well past teatime? Now, enough questions. I'm determined to get some decent grub into you two. It's bangers and mash for National Bangers and Mash Day."

Nan stood. Wiff and Dirty George popped up from the kitchen floor. The three of them embraced again.

"Off, the two of you. Go wash up," said Nan, maneuvering the boys to the downstairs bathroom. "I'll lay the table."

Wiff trudged down the hallway, dragging his rucksack, followed by his friend.

"Worm!" Dirty George shouted, remembering that he had a three-foot-long Madagascan worm living in his rucksack. He knelt down and tugged open his sack, and Worm spilled out, stretching to her full length, happy to be free of a cramped and sour-smelling old rucksack. "Thank God you're okay!" Dirty George shoved the back door wide and stepped outside. Boy and worm sank into a mound of dirt.

Wiff watched Dirty George and Worm playing in Nan's tiny garden; he could smell sausages cooking and hear eggs sputtering in the frying pan. Nan hummed. He could see Walrus curled like a comma in the old armchair beside the tall window overlooking the backyard.

In his head, Wiff made a list:

1. Avoid all trains to Brighton
2. Steer clear of Wolsey Warriors
3. Plant a garden for Nan
4. Tie the impossible knot
5. Keep an eye out for unusual-looking airships in the skies over London
6. Find a good spot in Diggs to hide the ZEBRA

Wiff spun around to go wash up, but tripped over his rucksack. He slid to the floor and dumped the contents in the hallway. A smelly assortment of articles tumbled out: a wad of paper, four soggy pieces of rope, a clump of matches, two empty sardine cans, a broken pencil. Wiff turned the rucksack over and gave it a good shake. A final object spilled out and spun across the stone floor. It was a stainless-steel ball, the size of a large marble. Wiff grabbed the sphere and held it in his open palm. The orb was warm to the touch and thrummed. He rolled the ball across his hand. Wiff froze when he saw that one side of the metal globe revealed an opening, like an eyeball, glowing red and pulsating, with the letter B.

"Blimey," Wiff gasped. "Basil's got an eye on us!"

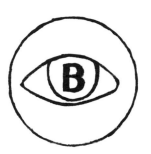

Wiff's Favorite Knots

Parts of a Rope

Working end: The tip or end of your rope that you're tying your knot

Standing part: The other end of your rope that you're not tying

Bight: The middle part of your rope

Knots

Bowline: A widely used loop knot

1. Take a long piece of working end and cross over the standing part to form a loop.

2. Pass the working end up through the loop, around the standing end, and back down the loop.

3. Pull the standing part with one hand and the two working ends with the other hand to tighten.

Clove hitch: A good knot for tying rope to a pole,
post, ring, or branch

1. Pass the working end of rope around the pole and cross under the standing part.

2. Pass the working end around the pole again to make a second turn.

3. Tuck the working end underneath the second turn.

4. Pull the working end and standing part to tighten.

Sheet bend: The most widely used knot for
joining two ropes

1. Take the rope on the left and make a loop.

2. Pass the working end of the rope on the right up through the loop, around the back of the loop rope, and back down the loop.

3. Tuck the working end under itself.

4. Pull the rope on the left and the working end of the right-hand rope to tighten.

Loop knot: This knot is also known as the slip noose or poacher's noose.

1. Form a loop by taking a long piece of working end back over the standing part.

2. Bring the working end under, over, and around the loop.

3. Pass the working end over the lower section of the loop created in step 2.

4. Pull the standing part to tighten.

Dirty George's Dictionary

Bangers and mash—sausages and mashed potatoes
Barmy—foolish
Bleedin'—an expression for something that is frustrating or bothersome
Blighter—an insignificant or objectionable person
Blimey—a mild exclamation
Blinking—an expression for something that is frustrating or bothersome
Bloke—man
Bloody—an expression for something that is frustrating or bothersome
Bonkers—crazy
Chap—man or boy
Cheeky—rude or sassy
Cheerio—good-bye
Cheers—good wishes or thanks
Chips—French fries
Cor—a mild exclamation
Crackers—crazy
Cracking—extremely or outstanding
Crikey—an exclamation expressing surprise
Daft—crazy
Diggs—lodgings
Dodge—a cunning trick
Dodgy—a dubious manner
Dole—unemployment money from the government
D.U.M.—Department of Underground Mischief
Dustbin—garbage can

Fab—fabulous or wonderful

Git—a silly or nasty person

Gobsmacked—utterly astonished or astounded

Gold Stick in Waiting—the Queen's assistant and protector

H.B.B.—His Basil's Barge

Kippers—a small salty fish

Knummers—no idea what this means because Wiff made it up

Larking—playing around or messing about

Loo—toilet

Lift—elevator

Mad—completely crazy

Menders—a repair shop

Me old cocker—term of endearment

Nick—to steal

Nutter—crazy

Oi—hey!

Pastie—a folded pastry filled with meat and vegetables

Plimsoles—sneakers

Pub—tavern or bar

Quid—pounds

Rucksack—backpack

Ruddy—an expression for something that is frustrating or bothersome

Smashing—excellent

Sweets—candy

Ta—thank you

Torchlight—flashlight

Twit—a silly or foolish person

Tyke—small child

Z.E.B.R.A.—Zipper Extraction Button Removal Atom-Smasher

About the Author

It took my mother, Lily, ten minutes to walk from 7 Wolsey Road to Marleyborne Hospital in North London. At eleven o'clock in the morning, on November 8, 1952, I came into the world.

My father worked on trains that delivered mail to distant places all over England. He wasn't there when I arrived. But that's where I get my love of trains.

We lived in a poor neighborhood of attached brick houses, narrow streets, and endless chimneys poking the sky. During World War II, a bomb from a German plane made a direct hit on the only pub on our street. One person was killed. They rebuilt the pub and called it The Lady Mildmay.

My best friend on Wolsey Road was an untidy boy named George. Mum called him Dirty George; she nicknamed me Wiff. It seems that neither of us cared much for soap and water. When I was almost eight, our family moved to the United States. We boarded the *Queen Elizabeth* in Southampton in southern England on April 21, 1960. We landed in New York City five days later.

I lost track of my English friend, went to college, married my sweetheart from New York, moved to Vermont, and grew up to write books. If you meet someone named George with a scruffy past, let me know.